THE DRAKKAN CHRONICLES

BOOK 1

THE

DARK SEA

BEYOND

RYE SOBO

COPYRIGHT

ISBN: 9781090541147

For Kristi

RYE SOBO

"Traveling - it leaves you speechless, then turns you into a storyteller."

\- IBN BATTUTA (1304-1377)

TABLE OF CONTENTS

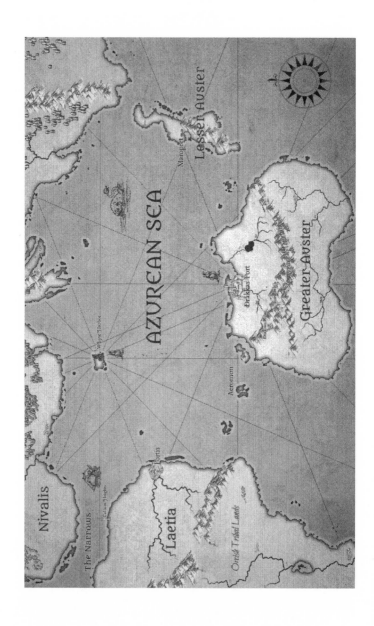

CHAPTER ONE

The gnome stood in the middle of the ancient Imperial Hall of the Black Keep, fresh blood dripped from his armor and covered his face.

"You have to understand, none of what happened, any of — this — was what I ever wanted," he stood with hands out to his side, blood fell from his fingers to the floor. He addressed the red-cloaked warrior-priests gathered before him.

"Apologies?" a priest asked as he tightened the grip on his glaive. "You can't just apologize and walk away from this."

At the center of the crimson phalanx stood a Dwarven woman, her hair and her beard the same fiery red as the armor she wore. Her eyes locked on

1

the blood-covered gnome before her. She clenched her jaw tight. Her fingers adjusted their grip on her scimitar, ready to deliver justice should her god demand it.

"Lusia—"

"Daen't. Ye will address us with the dignity and respect we deserve."

"Yes, you're right," he bowed his head and took a deep breath.

The thirty priests with their blades drawn were each capable of passing judgment on him. It was to her, only her, the gnome spoke. Her judgment was the only one that mattered. Only she could judge him for what he had done. For what he was about to do.

"Justiciars of Res, I am Ferrin Alsahar, wanted by you for murder and treason. I call upon my right as a Drakkan citizen to stand before you and plead my case."

"As a Drakkan?" Lusia scoffed at the absurdity. "Tell yer men to drop their arms and we'll grant ye an audience."

"I don't actually carry any weapons," a voice came from the stairwell. "And she kinda is a weapon on her own."

"Both of ye, get in here," Lusia said.

A tall, pale Elven man with shaggy brown hair dressed in flowing green robes stepped through the stairwell door. Ari held his hands out. "Very well. Very well."

Behind him stepped an orcish woman. Rook was dark-skinned like the gnome, but while he was brown, she had a greenish hue and large protruding lower teeth capped with iron. As she stepped from the stone doorway, the Dwarven war-priests stepped back to keep themselves out of her reach.

"Right," Lusia said. "Ye two sit down and daen't speak unless questioned. Understood?"

Ari and Rook nodded an agreement and sat in two chairs in the far corner of the Imperial Hall flanked by red-clad dwarves.

* * *

Ferrin knew how important today was. It had been years since he had seen his homeland, seen his family.

He closed his eyes and concentrated, remembered the fragrant scents of the spice merchant stalls in the Grand Arcade in the Market District. As he inhaled now all he smelled was smoke, ash, and blood.

Memories of the warm Drakkan sun on his face as he ran through the winding streets of the great walled city protected him from the harsh winter nights in the icy wildlands far away.

Even the tobacco Torsten smoked in the war camps reminded him of sitting on the floor of his father's study, reading tales of dragons, heroes, and great battles.

He worried if Lusia had been the right choice to judge him. He wondered what her opinion would be. As Ferrin, the foolish storyteller who ended up on the wrong side of the law, he could have asked her to pardon him and she would agree. But what would she say to a blood-soaked warlord in the heart of her city under siege?

* * *

Lusia sat in a high-backed chair just in front of the imperial throne. That chair, more imposing than its last occupant, had sat empty for over a hundred years. To either side, crimson dwarves pulled chairs from around the room and placed them on the dais, formed into a half-circle around the gnome.

Ferrin stood. He would be the center of attention and he always performed best standing.

"Are you ready?" he asked when the warriors settled.

Lusia nodded. "Ferrin Alsahar, do ye swear to tell the truth before this assembled panel and before Res, god of justice?" she asked with all the formality she could muster.

"May he strike me dead if a falsehood leaves my lips," Ferrin said.

"It's me that'll strike ye dead, Fer," Lusia said. She took a deep breath and nodded. "Then ye may begin when ye're ready."

"Right then," Ferrin said, "To tell this story I must tell it from the day I was forced from my home until this day, so that each of you may know the whole truth."

CHAPTER TWO

My head felt like a dragon sat on it.

"Where the hells am I?" I tried to keep silent while I stumbled around the room in search of a piece of furniture that wasn't moving.

I was at… The Stone Anchor Tavern. At the bar. I remember… pirates? My eyes focused in the darkened space.

A faint ray of morning sun slipped passed the fabric over a window. The chamber was luxurious but impersonal. It was the sterile comfort of a hotel room or tavern. *Somewhere in the Central Market, perhaps? It's far too nice to be Dockside.* It smelled of warm perfume, not saltwater and fish.

There was a girl… wasn't there? Shit. I turned around.

In bed next to me was a beautiful human woman. Young, perhaps in her early twenties.

Is she…? She's asleep. Good. Was she the pirate? Where are my clothes?

If I could find my clothes, I might slide out the door without disturbing her. On the chair I found my shirt and breeches. On top of the table I found my boots.

A chill ran through my naked gnomish body. *Shit.*

"Good morning my pirate captain," the woman said from the bed.

I was the pirate? I was within a step of the door. My breeches and shirt in one hand, boots in the other. I considered just bolting.

"Just heading to the galley to fetch some ale," I said.

"And coffee too. Please, Gustavo," she said with a pout.

"Certainly," I said with a smirk and stepped into the hallway.

Had she been awake, she would have noticed that I wasn't wearing trousers. She was still in the fantasy. Her pirate captain would pillage the tavern stores for her.

Keeping encounters like this short and mysterious is in her interest as much as mine.

The gentleman merchant leaving his room down the hall, however, was not in the fantasy. He was aghast at the bare-ass gnome trying with some difficulty to dress in the corridor.

I made my way to the end of the hall where I discovered a set of stairs, still uncertain of which establishment I was in. My head thrummed with each step.

At the bottom of the staircase I found a dining room and bar arranged for breakfast. Two people were in the room: the merchant I met in the hallway, who refused to make eye contact, and Norma, an older human woman who was the cook at the Compass Rose.

The Rose was a posh boarding house on the expensive side of the Market District. *That would explain the offense to a nude gnome. Wealthy travelers pay extra to avoid nonsense of that sort.*

"And what have we today?" Norma said with a wry smile. "Merchant lord with a flotilla of spice ships? Gallant hero just returned from a magnificent quest?"

"Pirate Captain Gustavo Blanco," I answered with a flourish.

Norma had often witnessed my early morning escapes. She understood the romantic fantasy, and on some level enjoyed her part in it.

"Oh my," she said with false astonishment, "how daring!"

The gentleman at the table let out an incredulous snort.

I put two iron pins on the bar. "Would you be so kind as to take the lady some coffee and pastries?" Then set a copper half knot down next to the pins, "and let her know —"

"The Watch drove you away from the premises, pursuing you like the villainous dog you are," she finished.

I smiled and turned for the exit.

"Good morning to you," Norma said, "Captain."

Outside the Compass Rose the city was already coming to life, if it ever slept. Merchants were setting up their stalls and farmers from south of the city were guiding herds of sheep and goats to the docks.

It was early in the harvest month of Panis and that was evident in the Central Market. Fresh fruits and vegetables were everywhere as I proceeded through the bustling crowds. The smell of fresh bread in dozens of nearby ovens mixed with fragrant spices and sweet fruity notes, filling the air with a pleasant, inviting quality.

On a street corner opposite the Grand Arcade, a justiciar, adorned in his red robes, prepared for the day. The older man, with dark brown skin and a white beard that reached to his navel, wore the dispassionate face of someone who had seen enough in his time that nothing surprised him anymore. Wisdom, I heard it described, though I considered it jaded.

Already a crowd had gathered to present grievances to the old man on the street corner.

Others to bear witness and hear the sordid details of their neighbors' lives.

* * *

Dem and I spent hours listening to the grievances as children. And hours more arguing with each other about the justiciar's rulings—how our ten-year-old's opinion differed from the judge. That passed as entertainment for us before women and whiskey. Instead, we would hear how Fawdil the mercer had cheated Loritus the tailor because he had used his young son's arm to measure the cubits of silk, shorting the order and ruining that wealthy merchant's shirt.

"They base a cubit on the person who is measuring," I argued as I stuffed a dried apricot into my mouth. "The mercer's apprentice couldn't use another hand to measure, only the one he had."

"But the tailor had ordered the silk from the mercer, not his son. Had the tailor known the child would do the measuring, he would have adjusted the order."

"If I was the apprentice, would you accuse me of cheating customers because of my gnomish stature?"

"I'm just glad I wasn't a tailor, a cubit of silk from you, Ferrin, wouldn't be enough for a single cuff," Dem said. Satisfied with his response he took an apricot from my hand and popped it into his mouth.

The justiciar, in his wisdom, ordered the mercer to replace the fabric with the correct measurements and to have a more watchful eye on the apprentice. Not long after that, the Council of Lords established a standardized cubit based on the Lord Regent's arm.

The grievances brought between friends, families, or spouses were always the most entertaining though.

My favorite was the case of Bakkar the baker, who accused his best friend, Samir the miller, of an adulterous relationship with his wife, because Bakkar saw Samir fleeing the family home early one morning.

"I would never betray my closest friend and brother by sleeping with his wife," the miller told the justiciar.

"But I saw him run from my family home, across the courtyard and over the garden wall before dawn, with nothing but the moonlight on his bare ass," the baker said. "Who then was he engaged without a thread of clothes? I ask my wife, but she will not look me in the eye! He is guilty, and she along with him."

I often laughed at the way people felt they needed to speak to the justiciar. It's as though he wouldn't understand if they didn't speak like the ancient poets.

"He was with me," announced the baker's mother after a long silence. "He was providing me with the comfort I had not had since my husband died two years earlier."

I still remember how the baker's face turned from a dark olive to a deep red as he realized the truth, he had caught his best friend sleeping not with his wife, but his mother.

"Comforting widows," that's how Dem would describe my exploits.

* * *

I snaked my way through the vendors in search of a morning meal, my heart set on some fresh apricots and goat cheese. The air of the market was sweet with apricots this morning, a fresh shipment must have arrived from Maropret overnight.

I glimpsed two men following me at a distance. They dressed well enough I could tell they weren't local cut-purses. *Most likely travelers.* Gnomes are a rare race outside the Auster Islands with only a few thousand in Drakkas Port.

I hoped to avoid the leers by sliding down an alley between stalls.

As I rounded the corner, one of the two men shouted, "That's him!"

I bolted, ran into the twisted thoroughfares of the Central Market, crouched under a counter, and through a carpet dealer's stall. I wasn't sure what these men thought I had done, but I knew I could never take both in a fight.

In the narrow confines of the Market my stature was a distinct advantage. I dashed into the market crossroads in front of the trading house and found two representatives of the Watch standing at the intersection. I stopped, struggling to catch my breath.

"Arrest that little devil," one man shouted to the Watch. The guards glanced down at me. My hands on my knees, chest heaving.

"What in the name of the gods is going on here?"

"I haven't done anything," I said.

"He's a pirate," the second traveler reported. "He absconded with my betrothed."

The guard looked down at me, "Pirate?"

I shrugged my shoulders. "Only time I've ever helmed a ship, it smashed into the wall and sank in the harbor."

"I remember that," the guard said excited. "Ten Hells, what a mess that was. Took a span to clear the Hydra's Mouth to anything bigger than a skiff."

"What's this about wife-stealing?" the other guard asked.

"She's not my wife, not yet. We were to be wed in two days' time," the traveler said. "He stole her away, forced himself on her, tainted our sacred union."

"Sounds like you haven't been union'ed yet," the guard said.

"A woman is free to do as she pleases, with whom she pleases," the second guard said. "You, however, are disrupting the peace and assaulting this man. I will ask you two to come with us, please."

The traveler scoffed. As the Watch approached, he threw out his arms to push off the armored men.

"Don't touch me, I will not go with you! Arrest him!"

The Watchmen grabbed the belligerent traveler and threw him to the ground. "You are now under arrest for attacking the Watch."

That had worked better than I expected.

The Watch lifted the man to his feet, his fresh clothes covered in dirt and manure, and frog-marched him through the streets toward the Black Keep.

I surveyed the area. I wasn't far from the Southern Empire. If I was quick and quiet, perhaps I could find a bite to eat.

CHAPTER THREE

The Southern Empire Trading Company headquarters was an enormous, three story building in the heart of the Central Market District. The modest white stucco walls, no different from much of the architecture of the city, exuded the well-crafted lie that the Southern Empire was just like every other trading house in the city.

Anyone with half a wit of sense knew the truth: many knew it as "The Empire" for a reason. The influence which originated here with the tiny proprietor stretched to the distant edges of the known world.

Over the massive timber-and-steel front door of the trading house was a large brass emblem of the company's crest. When I was a child, I wondered why no one had ever sought to steal the crest. It had to be worth a respectable fortune, at least several hundred silver heads as scrap.

With age and wisdom, I learned the reason that crest stood for generations of humans to see, there was no one in the Commonwealth foolish enough to buy the crest off a would-be thief. It meant having to deal with Zori's wrath.

Zori inherited Fritzbink & Sons around the time the Fortean Empire disintegrated. Her father never came to grips with the fact he only had a single daughter. Zori represented the "and Sons" of the company.

The collapse of the Fortean Empire was one of conflict and confusion across the Auster Islands, which comprised most of the protectorates of the empire. With the collapse, the currency became worthless and many trading houses fell with the empire.

My mother told me during those times a loaf of bread cost five silver, a month's wages. People starved. Livestock butchered and seed grain eaten just to keep families fed. Many found themselves outside the gates of the Temple District begging for scraps of anything to eat and a few coins. It was because of these bleak times that the Commonwealth adopted the outstretched hands on the silver palms coin, to remind us of when Drakkans had to beg.

Any other merchant would have sold their ships and hawked their inventories. Many of them did. Zori, who was into her second century by then, sought adventure. She bought whole trading houses and used her new fleet to transport food, weapons,

and mercenaries into the city from farms in Lesser
Auster. She smuggled out the Fortean noblemen and
their households who were escaping from the roving
companies of mercenaries looting the city.

It's claimed, though never substantiated, that Zori
got a quarter of everything raided from manors in
the Gilded Hill and half the coin any noble tried to
flee with. In the tumult, Zori thrived.

Over the next hundred years after the downfall of
the Empire, the turmoil settled. Zori had a second
son, changed the name of the business, and
established shops in every major city along the
Azurean coasts.

I slid through the massive main door of the
Southern Empire Trading Company and through the
corridors of clerks and money-counters to the
warehouse in the rear. At just two cubits tall, I could
walk full-upright past the counters and not be seen
over the piles of paperwork.

*This late in the harvest season the storehouse must be
filled with crates of produce and dried meats ready to ship
to the Outer Islands soon. She won't miss a few items.*

Zori stood on top of a wooden crate to be eye level
with a dark, thin man in the uniform of a merchant
captain. She made a point, despite her gnomish
stature, to furnish the Empire offices for the
convenience of her human clients and employees.

Zori and the captain were at a table in the middle
of the warehouse checking manifests and charts.

Captain Claudio Azpa listened to his master while he poured over the documents.

"One in each of the offices," she said. "The station manager will have the key, which will need to be sent on a separate ship."

"As you wish," Captain Azpa said in his smooth, thick Laetian accent. "Should the recipient be informed of delivery?"

"They will know when the time is right. There's no need to arouse suspicions," she said.

Keeping one eye on the two merchants, I opened a crate with only the faintest of creaks, slid my hand into the container and removed a massive, cured sausage.

"Do you plan on working today, Ferrin," Zori asked without glancing up from the table. "Or just stealing my wares?"

I froze, sausage half tucked into my trousers, hesitant to say anything. I stood. There was no sense hiding from Zori.

"I still have need of another deckhand," the captain said. "Perhaps he can earn back what he has stolen."

Zori nodded.

"Claudio's ship leaves port tonight," Zori said. "Two spans to Whyte Harbor and back."

"Forty days!" I protested. "I really have so much to do."

"Oh? What's her name?" Zori asked.

"I don't know yet," I said. "I mean, the options are endless these days—"

"The *Delilah Fritzbink*. Shouldn't be too difficult for you to remember," she said cutting me off. "It's named after your grandmother. Now if you're not working, get the hell out of my storehouse."

I adjusted the sausage in my pants and pushed my way through the crates toward the door.

"Tonight," I said. "I'll let you know."

Had anyone else intruded, Zori Alsahar would have had the thief drawn and quartered. But as her son, I got offered a month-long job. To this day, I'm still uncertain which fate was worse.

CHAPTER FOUR

I stepped out of the Southern Empire to ponder the offer from my mother. *Four spans.* The longest I'd ever been away from Drakkas Port was a span and a half.

Even then, that was an overland trip to the Stormreach Mountains with my father and brother. Forty days at sea?

I squatted on the broad stone steps of the Empire's trading house and stared out over the city.

The glistening harbor opened to the north of the Central Market with hundreds of ships crowded together in a chaotic swarm that only the most seasoned sailors could follow. The Harbor Master's Tower stood at the center of the crescent moon that made up the docks surrounding the harbor.

Across the crowded thoroughfare from the Harbor Master's Tower was the shrine to Aequor, the god of the sea, with its spiraled dome and imposing stone spires.

The western half of the crescent moon was an amalgam of storehouses, bars, and brothels frequented by the perpetual stream of merchants entering and departing the port. The eastern half dedicated to naval docks, shipwrights, bars, and brothels. Fort Hydrus, the ancient stronghold of the city, climbed above the eastern docks and dominated the northeastern quarter.

Opposite the fort, the northwestern part of the city was Smuggler's Scourge, with its tight serpentine corridors and network of ramshackle homes. Built from the scraps of ships, crates, canvas, and everything else residents could get their hands on. The shacks of the Scourge climbed the gigantic stones of the imposing outer walls like *Monkey Vines* consuming a mighty *Barno* tree.

The surrounding streets grew dark. The shadow of something massive blocked out the sun over the city. I glanced up just in time to meet the head of an immense, red, mountain dragon gliding without a sound fifty feet above the roof of the Empire. Then another and another. In all five massive lizards clad in steel, each larger than three ships placed bow-to-stern, circled above the Black Keep before turning and diving toward the fortress. The famed dragon vanguard of the Drakkan Commonwealth, protectors of Drakkas Port for at least two thousand years.

The vanguard traveled with the Drakkan army when it deployed, working as something of a blend between a scouting force and "a flying wall of fire-breathing holy fuck, putting the fear of Cassis into our enemies," as Dem always characterized them. It had been a year since I had seen the vanguard. The Council had committed a substantial detachment of the army to Laetia, for reasons never made clear to the citizens of the Commonwealth.

The dragons fly quicker than the ships, so they will island hop as the ships transporting the army advance from the Auster Islands to Laetia, allowing the dragons plenty of chance to rest and eat. Once the flotilla is within a day of the capital, the dragons fly home. The early morning flyover and the southern approach means they stayed the night in Dragons' Roost in the Stormreach Mountains.

It also meant the fleet would arrive by midday. A few thousand soldiers returning from a year abroad, heavy with coin, meant the liquors would flow and new stories abound.

Roused from my thoughts, I pressed my way north through the teeming market. There was a fresh vitality in the crowd, perhaps from the sight of the battle-dragons flying overhead, perhaps from the prospect of family members home from distant shores. As I worked through Central Market, I noticed merchants raising crimson and gold pennants above their stalls and hanging fresh bunting in the Commonwealth's colors from the trade halls and boarding houses.

The priests in the Temple District say Cassis, the god of war, and Pecunia, the goddess of commerce, are twins. As one sibling prospers, the other also has their fill. As I watched the merchants move in an excited flurry, it was easy to understand the truth in that belief. By the end of the span, the coins from the fort will have progressed to the purses of every mercer, miller, grocer, whore, and barkeep in the city. Soon, everyone would have their stake of the spoils — everyone but the soldiers.

The excited energy of the Central Market turned to frenetic action Dockside. Stevedores moved from one dock to the next, carried mooring lines, hooks, and crates toward the eastern side of the wharf.

In the far distance, near the walls of the citadel, the priests in the temple of Cassis had stoked fires and heavy white columns of smoke ascended from the fresh sacrifices being performed. The head of one of the massive wyrms peered above the wall of Fort Hydrus as it heaved a sheep into the air before devouring it whole.

Men, dark from a lifetime of days under the hot Drakkan sun, led mules and carts at a brisk pace from warehouses to the berths, weighted down with cargo intended for ships on the western side of the harbor. There was a crowd clustered around the Harbor Master's Tower as ships' officers scrambled to change departure times to set sail before the Hydra's Mouth became choked with the hundred warships that would soon flood into the harbor.

The towering walls defended the capital from attack, but the city runs on commerce. To secure the port and the critical shipping, the architects of the Great Walls of Drakkas Port extended the one-hundred-foot-tall walls into the harbor, and provided only a narrow break, wide enough for an individual ship to pass through, as the sole means of entering or exiting the harbor. This challenge left the Harbor Master to organize the hundreds of ships that passed through the Hydra's Mouth on any span. With the fleet returning, warships would block the Mouth until well after dark. Any captain hoping to escape before nightfall would need to leave in the next few turns at the latest.

I turned left past the temple of Aequor and followed the busy half-moon seawall around to the three-story stone and mud building which looked as though it had collapsed on several occasions and the occupants had just stacked the stones back up where they thought they should go. On the facade, someone had driven a corroded navigator's sextant into the mudwork above the door. The building had no other markings, except the sign that identified the decrepit building as a public house. The denizens of the dilapidated hall all knew it as the Rusted Sextant.

CHAPTER FIVE

From within the Sextant, the atmosphere was everything one would expect in a questionable tavern along the harbor. The air was always thick with the smell of cheap tobacco, cheaper booze, fish, and the dank, salty air of the sea. The few windows in the place were caked with decades of dust, vomit, and blood, so the place had the feel of twilight even at midday. A dozen or so tables in various states of collapse were littered around the main room with an assortment of broken chairs and crates pulled alongside them. At that early hour, the Sextant had nearly emptied of the crowd that had passed out the night before.

"Fer'n! You see 'em?" Max said.

Maximilian sat behind the ancient, beer encrusted bar and slowly sipped on a cup of bilge water he insisted was quality Aeromon-style coffee.

"See what? Did something happen?" I played dumb.

Max, like most people who did not grow up in Drakkas Port, was always excited to see the dragons circle overhead. His face lit up like a child watching an illusionist's play during the Festival of Arkanus. How could I possibly take that from him with a jaded response?

"Drag'ns! The fleet'll be in soon," he said. "Tonight, all the docks will be a huge party! We'll get rich!"

"What? You mean we're not getting rich off all these drunken adventurers," I said with a grand flourish of the room.

In total there were eight people in the Sextant that morning: Max, me, Old Herus nursing the hair of the dog, and five men clad in a random collection of armor. The Rusted Sextant saw its share of adventurers fresh from their travels, mostly because the cheap rooms and cheaper booze. They were the reason I frequented the run-down pub with such regularity. Adventurers bring with them stories of adventure, or failed adventure, or attempted adventure — stories I used to relish hearing as a young boy.

Greater Auster has been continuously inhabited for close to four thousand years. The Fortean Empire built fortresses and temples, now mostly in ruin, across the island during their two-thousand-year run of the place, and Auster was the only place ever known to have domesticated a dragon, if you can consider a flying wall of fire-breathing death in plate armor to be domesticated. The island was ripe for the adventuring sort. These five men: a human, a half-elf, two dwarves, and an honest-to-goodness high elf made up the latest in a long tradition of post exploration debauchery.

If there is anything rarer in Commonwealth than a gnome, it's a high elf. At one time, when the empire ruled the Azurean Sea, the high elves had a substantial settlement in the capital city, Fortis. But when the empire began to collapse, the elves fled. Perhaps back to Jia, beyond the Caligin Ocean. Their offspring with the humans were common enough. You could find half-elves, or quarter-elves in most port towns, but a full-blooded high elf was a rare sight indeed.

"We're nae drunk yet," one of the dwarves said in response to my flourish. "Nae with this swill."

"Speafer yaselph," Old Herus slurred from his spot at the bar.

"Max, these lads are looking for quality beverages," I said. "Grab that bottle of Stormreach Whiskey from under the counter, please." I knew that happy customers with a few strong drinks in them could share some stories.

"That's much better. Thank ye, lad," the dwarf said.

I pulled a crate close to the adventurers' table. Up close they wore the signs of battle. The dwarves each had singed beards. The half-elf had a makeshift bandage wrapped around his bicep and dried blood ran down his arm. The human had a squared dent in the center of his breastplate, where he had clearly taken a warhammer to the chest.

"You look like you had a hell of a time," I said. "I'd hate to see the other guys!"

"If you do, be sure to slit their throats for us," the human said.

Max came up to the table and set down seven glasses and provided a healthy pour into each. "What're we drinking to then?"

"Seamus," the high elf said in a graveled voice, grabbing a glass and raising it up without breaking eye contact with the table.

"Aye, to Seamus," one of the dwarves said. "May Lady Nex keep him." The men each grabbed a glass and raised it in their friend's honor. Max shot me a knowing glance as he raised his glass, downed the drink, and returned to the bar.

After a long, uncomfortable silence, the human looked over to me. "Do you know anywhere we could get some armor repaired?"

"You mean that dent," I said pointing to the concaved breastplate, "I can fix that."

"You?" he asked with an incredulous look.

"Take it off and put it here on the crate," I said as I grabbed a glass and walked over to the fireplace. I half-filled the glass with Max's bilge-coffee from a kettle resting on the hearth near the fire. The rest of the party laughed as the human pulled at the straps of the armor.

"Would a gnome even know what to do with armor?" asked the half-elf with a laugh. "He's likely to turn it into a boat and float out of here."

"Aye, with my cock as the rudder," I said as I returned to the armor at the crate.

I slid the hot glass under the breastplate. The high elf cocked his head to the side and watched me with intense scrutiny. I closed my eyes and began to focus on the boiling liquid in the glass. Placing my hand on the steel just above the glass, I took a deep breath, muttered an arcane word, and pulled my fist into the air.

THUD. I opened my eyes to see the armor reshaped back into its original form without a hint of the mighty hammer blow that had been there a moment ago. I picked up the plate mail and handed it back to its owner who, along with the other party members, had gone from laughter to stunned silence.

"I guess I'm going to need another boat," I said.

The human, wide-eyed, took the armor back from me and looked it over. Content with the work he reached into his purse and handed me four silver palms, about twice what Max pays me a week for entertaining the customers.

I had spent enough time around adventurers to know that there was no story to be gleaned from them. Most likely they were ambushed by bandits before they ever got near the ruins. The bandits probably mistook the dwarves for mercenaries from Stormreach and thought they had a good score.

In the ensuing scuffle, Seamus charged the attackers. By the look on the high elf's face during the toast, I guess he cast a fireball that enveloped the bandits and Seamus. The dwarves tried to pull their friend back, but the flames were just too much for them. Their beards and tabards were singed.

The human was likely the ringleader of the expedition. He probably told his friends that it would be easy. They could just find an old temple and dig around for some treasure. The quiet dwarf blamed the human for Seamus's death. He was the one who had sunk his warhammer, which he had tried to hide under his pack, into the human's chest.

This was an expedition that had failed miserably. That was the look Max had shot me. He had read the scene as soon as he approached.

I sighed.

The icy cold glass burned my fingers as I picked it up and turned toward the bar. A light hand touched my shoulder. I turned to see the high elf, now stooping to look me in the face.

"I would not have expected to see such a skilled arcanist in a place such as this," the elf said in his deep, graveled voice. "Your efficiency is impressive."

"Thank you," I said, a bit dumbfounded. I knew that a compliment of any kind from a high elf was as rare as a unicorn, but a high elf complimenting another's manipulation of the Fabric was something that just didn't happen. The whiskey must have already had its effect on the elf. "I studied for a number of years under my father at the University. That's the extent of my parlor tricks."

I politely nodded and made my way to the bar to pour out the nearly frozen bilge-coffee.

The high elf returned the nod and rejoined his companions who were still chattering about the armor.

Behind the bar, I looked up at Max. "I know," I said. "I just—"

BWONG. A thunderous gong rang out across the harbor outside.

"They're here," Max said as his look of concern disappeared. The excited child returned.

CHAPTER SIX

I ran to the doorway and squinted out into the bright sunlight of the harbor. A second gong hit reverberated out from the Harbor Master's Tower. This time the low bellow of a war horn from some place deep inside the citadel followed.

Centuries ago, the sailors of the city devised this means of signaling the Watch of an incoming warship. The gong would sound to alert the citizens, to rally men to arms. If the soldiers in Fort Hydrus expected the ships, the horn signaled the Harbor Master to grant the vessels entry. If the gong sounded and no horns, it was an unmistakable warning to every resident that the city was being invaded.

At least, that's the intention. It's more of a formality, a part of the ceremony of the returning fleet. The Harbor Master's apprentice had devoted the last span practicing the run to the top of the tower, removing the large mallet from an ornate wooden box inlaid with gold, and striking the muffled gong as hard as he could. The striking of the gong to welcome the fleet for the first time would be a monumental day in his young career. As long as the gong has been in the tower, no one has struck it without the accompanying horn. No nation has ever tried to invade the city, at least not since the Forteans first landed in a tiny fishing village over two thousand years ago.

My attention, along with most everyone in Drakkas Port, shot from the tower to the Hydra's Mouth. Despite having seen the fleet return dozens of times before, I always felt the surge of excitement at seeing the great warships decorated with flags and shields gliding into the harbor, one after another.

I watched the gap in the colossal wall and held my breath in anticipation. Cheers erupted from near the Harbor Master's Tower as they first glimpsed the returning warship. Soon enough, an immense golden dragon head pierced through the breach in the wall. It was the figurehead of the *Fortune*, the flagship of the Commonwealth's navy. On board, officers dressed in their finest uniforms, donned solely for celebrations such as this, and stood triumphant on the decks of the ship.

From this distance I could only make out the plumage of the officers' helmets. It was a glorious procession of peacocks perched atop a golden dragon.

Crowds of people spilled from the city onto the central and western docks. The roar grew louder as the masts of the man-of-war passed the great stone walls. Enterprising merchants went up and down the seawall, hawking sausages and meats-on-sticks and crimson and gold flags.

Everyone made money when the fleet returned home.

The flock of peacocks veered toward the east as the *Fortune* found its berth in the center of the docks, near the gates to Fort Hydrus. The crowd cheered again as the next flock entered the harbor.

Ship after ship, the parade of military vessels entered the port as longshoremen scurried across the harbor like ants swarming a dropped pastry. The ships packed tight into the harbor, the largest ships closest to the fortress and the smaller ships around the outside.

Soon there were fewer peacocks and the red tunics of the army were most prominent on the decks.

The exuberant cries of the crowds when the *Fortune* arrived turned into a rising and falling din as the novelty wore off.

Max stood beside me, a flag in one hand and meat-on-a-stick in the other. He still cheered as each smaller ship entered the harbor.

"Who's taking care of the Sextant?"

"Herus."

"Can he even see straight?"

"Not sure he ever could."

"And the adventurers?"

"Drank yer supply, I'm not so worried 'bout'em," Max said. "What're they gonna take?"

I shrugged.

The ships on the western side came to life once more as the merchant ships, held up by the processional, could disembark.

The sun dropped behind the outer stone walls. The crowd dispersed back up into the city. The usual wharf rats and prostitutes replaced the families on the docks.

Here and there a red tunic appeared along the seawall. Then a few more. The steady stream of red ran down the dock from Fort Hydrus and across the capital.

I headed back to the Sextant to find a few of the tables filling up. Behind the bar where Max was filling ceramic tankards with cheap ale, I pulled my pathetic excuse for an *oud* from the corner. I had learned to play while attending the University and had become proficient in the few decades I was there.

The *oud* in the Sextant, however, was far from the instrument I had played in school, finely-crafted and made of warm *Barno* wood. Two of the eleven strings on this instrument were missing, their tensioners broken off by an earlier musician. There was a split up the neck where Max had thrown a drunkard against the wall and the *oud* had cushioned the impact.

In all honesty, I hadn't tuned the thing in at least two spans and it produced a hideous noise. Given the option between this thing and a pair of rusty spoons, any musician worth two iron pins would consider the benefits of tetanus.

Which is how it happened to be in my possession, the last owner died of lockjaw.

I did little more than strum a harsh chord to get a song started or draw the attention of the crowd before launching into a story, so I cared little what sound it produced, so long as it produced one.

I clambered on top of the bar, drew the *oud* up in front of me, and struck the remaining strings with a *THWANG*. The sour note elicited an explosion of laughter from the room. Good, they were already in high spirits. I patted the *oud* as though it were a shamed pet and slipped it behind my back. I stomped on the bar and started a rousing first verse of *Sweet Drakkan Ladies*. By the time I arrived at the chorus, the crowd joined in.

It's going to be a good night.

CHAPTER SEVEN

The Sextant was far down the western side of the harbor which meant it was well into the evening before the red tunics of the soldiers filtered into the tavern. On any other night I would have played a few songs and departed with a few half-knots to find something better to invest my time on than work. With the return of the fleet the coin was flowing. I had already made a month's earnings before I told tales of the daring exploits of Ferrin the Great. At the Sextant, this passed as comedy.

In all recorded history, there had never been a single gnomish soldier — too small for the arms and armor. A gnome had never explored an ancient temple, other than a research trip. In fact, the most excitement a gnome had ever encountered was when

Zori smuggled nobles out of the city a hundred years ago. But despite my lack of aptitude for adventure, I could craft the most exciting tales of heroism out of the parts of failed adventures.

Yes, I, Ferrin Alsahar, ripped off the accounts of every traveler to pass through the Sextant and wove myself into the starring role. That night, I had a fresh story of would-be adventure.

THWANG.

> *Sisters of Erista four, allow me to tell of Ferrin's lore: The mighty hero, adventuring gnome, trav'ling the wilds of Auster his home. For the enjoyment of all who join in this roar.*

The crowd was already in an intoxicated frenzy when I started my second set with a classic invocation to the goddess of arts and her sisters the muses. Cheers broke out as I went into my usual bawdy tales.

> *Deep in the dark woods of the Forbidden Forest, beyond the lake where the night hag lies, there is a temple all but forgotten, to Muscan, dark god of the flies. Within the temple there is said to be a massive golden horde amassed by Varenax, an ancient Fortean lord known for being wealthy, and cruel, and wise.*

> *But this is not a tale of Varenax, no this is a story that starts with this ember and grows into the inferno of an epic of how Ferrin the Great defeated a gang of bandits with his obscenely large member. With a wash basin on his chest and sauce pan for a helm upon his head, he was truly a force to reckon with, filling his foes with a dread. Listen*

close to what I say, it is something you'll want to remember.

The fated five who traveled from a faraway shore sought riches and gold and the love of a Drakkan whore. But barely a day from the Great Gate they had ridden when they were set upon by a band of thieves laying silently hidden behind the boulders and rocks that dotted the moor.

This party was new, not adventurers yet. A banker, a butcher, a scholar there too, a mercer and tanner completed the set. Outfitted in the finest they could never afford; their armor was held together with twine and with cord. None trusted the other, they had only just met.

From a distant rise Ferrin watched the approach, stunned to see adventurers out riding in a coach. To bandits this must have appeared a wonderful thing, a morning ride of some baron or king. But these travelers were pinless, without so much as a half knot to poach.

So, from far afield Ferrin now flew, the gnome racing with a speed hardly any knew. For the smallest of all men are the fastest as well, though preferring comfort you never could tell that the secret to their speed is that they are running on three legs, not two.

The gnome was too fast for the brigands to block; as Ferrin drew close, the thieves he did mock. Clashing of armor as the ruffians fell, a flurry of blows too fast to tell what had happened to the bandits until the leader dropped too, bludgeoned to death by the gnome's mighty cock.

The crowd exploded in cheers and laughter at the punchline of the story. The Rusted Sextant was a rough bar, packed with old salts, whores, soldiers, and drunks. They were the type of characters that never grew tired of my stories, which often included bludgeoning evildoers with my impractically over-sized member.

As the great Fortean playwright Alonzo Pyrell once said, a stereotype that flatters should always be perpetuated for poetic purposes.

✳ ✳ ✳

The door of the Sextant flew open with a crash. Three men in glistening armor pushed their way into the cramped common room.

"Alright, nobody moves," roared the lead man as more of his comrades pushed into the tavern.

At the order, several patrons near the bar turned and bolted for the back door, not wanting a run-in with the Watch.

"We're searching for the pirate captain Gustavo Blanco. We know he's here, so surrender him at once," said the soldier at the front of the phalanx formed in the heart of the pub.

"Seven men to capture one gnome," I said with a smirk. "You'd think the Watch would at least make it a fair fight!"

Nervous laughter rippled through the crowd, as they braced to see a bloody brawl. From my vantage point, I could see a few men pull daggers from their boots. Most of the patrons of the Sextant were far too inebriated to realize that these intruders had the red tunics of the army under their armor, not the grey tunics of the Watch.

That bastard thinks he's got the upper hand. He thinks he can saunter into my bar and shout orders.

I reached down and unfastened the top button of my breeches and slid out the massive, cured sausage I had pilfered earlier in the day. Agnes, one of the regular barmaids at the Sextant, howled in encouragement and a roar of laughter again erupted from the Sextant.

"Howdafuck duziwalk with that," Old Herus mumbled from his chair at the bar, awestruck by what he was certain he witnessed.

The line of soldiers broke and from behind them an officer doubled over in laughter. "Erista be damned, Ferrin! Put that thing away," he shouted.

Dem pulled off his shining plumed helmet and set it on the bar revealing his reddened face with tears streaming down his cheeks. His olive complexion had darkened from a year in the sun and his soot black hair was cropped short in the fashion popular with the soldiers.

Turning to his men, still laughing, Dem tossed a small purse to the door-kicker. "First round is on me, boys, good work."

The soldiers all cheered, removed their helmets, and pressed toward Max at the bar.

Realizing they would not get the fight they had expected, the denizens of the Rusted Sextant returned to the laughter and debates over who thought my prop was real.

"What the hell did you do to that poor goose, Dem?" I asked, pointing to the gleaming steel helmet on the bar with a cluster of golden feathers protruding from the pointed crown.

"That's Commander to you, sir," he said, as he puffed up his chest and stuck out his chin.

"Were they drunk?" I asked.

Dem sneered at me.

"Max, a bottle of the good stuff for the Commander." I let the word hang in the air. I had known Dem for my entire life. We were best mates growing up. The first person to agree to whatever insane idea I had dreamed up. I was there the day he enlisted, almost ten years earlier. He would always tell me the stories of his campaigns around Laetia and the Outer Islands. Now he was a commander, and I was still telling cock jokes in a seedy tavern.

"An Alsahar spending coin? That's a first!" Dem said with mock astonishment. "Better make it two, Max. I don't know when I'll get the opportunity again!"

Max set two bottles of Stormreach Whiskey on the bar and two glasses. I set a silver palm on the counter next to the bottles, the outstretched hands on the coin reaching out pleading. Max slid the coin across the bar, smiled, and tucked it into his pocket, "Welcome home, Commander."

With a well-practiced nod, Dem took up the bottles and glasses and looked down with a warm

41

smile, "So are you still working, or do you have time for a drink?"

"After the stunt you pulled? I can't follow that. There's a table back here that opened by the back door when you barged in."

We pushed our way through the crowded room to the back of the hall. A half-broken table with one good chair and an empty crate was abandoned by the door. Dem grabbed the chair and slid it around so his back was against the wall. I hopped up on the wooden crate and poured healthy servings of dwarven whiskey.

"So how are the widows of Drakkas Port?" Dem asked with a smirk on his face. "Well comforted, I hope."

"I was nearly gutted in the Central Market this morning," I said. "Some beautiful young orphan I was comforting all last night forgot to mention she was on her way to be married today. Her betrothed and his brother didn't take too kindly to the substantial philanthropy I had provided.

Dem roared with laughter.

"But seriously, how did you swing commander?" I slid a glass with four gnome-fingers of whiskey across the half-table. "When I last saw you, you were a sergeant. Now you have a half a duck stuck to your head."

"Luck, mostly…misfortune? I don't know what to call it," Dem said as he sipped on the smooth, oaky drink, staring off through the table in the way he always did when he came back from a deployment.

"Captain Marcellus developed a fever during the voyage to Laetia. By the time we reached Fortis, Lady Nex keep him, he was gone. General Aurellis appointed me Captain."

"By her frozen hands," I said, regretting I had brought up the subject. "I—I'm sorry."

"It happens," he said in a nonchalant tone. "The sea is dangerous. We all know it. Sometimes we win, sometimes it does. That's how it goes."

He looked me square in my eyes. There was an intensity I rarely saw in Dem, "We all know the price."

"So, what happened once you got to Laetia?" I asked. He was holding something back. A part of me didn't want to know. But a much larger part was bouncing up and down.

I always got my best material from Dem.

CHAPTER EIGHT

"**W**e deployed to northern Laetia, a request from the Fortean Council to aid with an incursion," Dem said, as his focus shifted from me to the table and through the table to somewhere far off.

"The Forteans said they were being invaded, a force of perhaps a hundred thousand, from across the Narrows from Nivalis. A movement of troops on that scale hadn't occurred since the Collapse.

Fifty thousand strong and five dragons, we were to reinforce the garrison at Callum Heights, an old Fortean fortress atop a seventy-foot cliff that overlooked the Narrows. If the Nivs were coming over the Narrows, we would make them pay to do it."

"That doesn't make sense," I said. "Why would the Commonwealth send troops to defend Fortis from an invasion? Why not let the Forteans defend their own land?"

"Because Fortis is one of the largest nations in the world, and our best trading partner," Dem said. "And because less than three generations ago, WE were Forteans."

"Human generations," I corrected. "Ma and Pa survived the Collapse, Duk too."

"You're just proving my point, Ferrin. Zori and Ignis, Dukhan, many gnomes and elves alive today were born Forteans. You can't just turn your back on them," Dem said, "especially if what the Forteans were saying was true. If the Nivs really were invading."

"Were they?"

"Did I interrupt your story?"

"Actually," I said with a wave around the common room filled with soldiers.

"So anyway," Dem continued, ignoring my gesticulations. "We arrived in Callum Heights in early Cienta last year after over seven spans on the ships. And there's nothing there. We had expected an army encampment, a fleet off the coast, something. But there was nothing—a quiet fishing village and the old Fortean fortress with a garrison of a thousand soldiers.

"General Aurellis stormed up to the gates of the fortress with half the officer corps in tow. He pounded his fists on the gates as if he was the war god Cassis himself. He demanded entry, said he would 'sunder the whole damned rock pile,' if he didn't get answers.

"A pudgy half-orc named Starrik was the garrison's commander. He brought Aurellis and the rest of us up to the battlements. Looking over, he pointed to the fishing village down the beach from where our landing skiffs were beached. Starrik said three months earlier, there was nothing here. The village and all its inhabitants were Nivs, washed up on the beach and made an encampment that grew and grew. There were supposed to be two other camps further west just as big as the one near the fort. I swear Aurellis nearly threw that mixed *verdi* bastard right off the battlement.

"We took four days and nights to disembark. Since there was no enemy army, we built our encampment on the highlands around the southern side of the fortress. Over a few months, Callum Heights had gone from a desolate outpost on the farthest reaches of Laetia to a tent city with as many residents as Fortis or Drakkas Port.

"They tasked me with construction of palisades around our encampment, if the Nivs were hostile, we needed to hold them back at least long enough to fall back into the fortress. With housing and support services tended to, we needed to find out what had driven the ice-eaters to brave the chaotic waters of the Narrows to Laetia.

"On our fifth day, General Aurellis assembled the officer corps at the fort. He split the army into three, one for each Niv encampment along the coast. They dubbed the camps Lar, Fida, and Carnum, after the deities of the home, truth, and health, respectively.

"Commander Lorenzo Rayner, my commanding officer, would assume the title of Commandant to oversee coordination between the three armies. My feet ached at the thought of the endless miles I was about to undertake, running back and forth between the three encampments. Two months on a barge. A war that never came. Now I was a messenger. It could have been worse.

"Commander Gaius Laudon was placed in command of the First Army. He would oversee Encampment Lar, the western most camp, about a day's march from the fortress. Commander Remus Stormjaw, a fierce dwarven tactician, took command of the Second Army at Encampment Fida, the center of this new trail of cities. And then the General bellowed a line I'll never forget. 'Commander Demetric Pictus will take the Third Army to Carnum.'"

"I was as slack-jawed then as you are now, Fer. I left Drakkas Port a grunt with a handful of rookies that looked up to me. I knew nothing of how to command an army. I could lay siege to a city of forty thousand, but run one?"

"I took a small detachment with me the first time I entered Carnum. I don't think I'll ever forget the sights or the smell — raw sewage, disease, and death. Gaunt women, flesh pulled tight against their bones, wrapped in the furs of mangy creatures. Pale children, only half clothed, ran through waste that flowed in channels between the makeshift hovels of the town. They constructed houses from driftwood, sail fragments, parts of the boats they had arrived on, and anything else they could scavenge from the surrounding area. Carnum made Smuggler's Scourge look like the Gilded Hill. Make no mistake, when I hear the clerics speak of the depths of the Ten Hells, I think of what I saw on that shore."

Dem sat dead still for a long, painful moment. His eyes sliced through the floor to somewhere else. I sat in silence, waiting for my friend to return as I had done so many times.

"I—" Dem struggled for the words, "I had to help them as best I could."

"I know you did," I said. "Because that's who you are. You're a good man."

Dem tossed back his whiskey and wiped his face with his hand. He poured himself another four fingers, looked at me, and nodded.

"I set two units to digging a channel from the encampment to the sea. We used the tides to flush the filth out of the channels between buildings. There were four columns of healers attached to the Third Army, I had ordered them to work their way through the camp doing what they could to comfort the sick and dying. We dedicated six columns of men to building pyres higher up the beach to begin the grim task of handling the scores of dead.

"After setting the duties I found the healers in the mess hall. Grabbing one by his armor, I demanded to know why they weren't in the encampment as I had ordered. Another of the healers spoke first, said the

Nivs turned them away, shouting, screaming about 'The Darkness.' These were simple folk. They were afraid of the arcanists, or so I thought.

"I returned to the encampment with a single column of healers, ten medics proficient in healing without magic. An old woman wielding a large carving knife, the kind the rangers used to field dress deer before bringing them back to camp, met us at the edge of the encampment.

"Her name was Baba Kerushk, a de facto matriarch for the encampment. She pointed the large blade at the healers, their white tunics caked in mud and filth.

"'No magic,' I explained to her. I kept my hands outstretched to show her I meant no harm. 'But I want medics to look after the sick.'

"To my surprise, the old Niv spoke a formal dialect of Imperial with a thick accent. 'Healers may tend to the sick, but the arcane may not touch the dead,' she said. 'We have seen The Darkness.'

"I explained that none of the men with me were arcanists. She nodded and waved them forward with her large knife. I asked her what she meant by 'having seen The Darkness.' It was what they called whatever they were fleeing from.

"According to Baba Kerushk, an army of malevolent forces was marching down from the far north across Nivalis. This force, The Darkness, brought unspeakable violence. Entire cities overrun, slaughtered to the man or submitted to the force. She mentioned Niv men from one town being forced to attack the next. Word of this army spread far across the continent.

"One day, a runner said The Darkness was a day from Baba Kerushk's village. Her sons vowed to stay and fight. She took the women and children and ran. They did not stop running until they reached the sea where they found thousands more fleeing for their lives.

"In a rotted skiff with forty other Nivs, she pushed off into the Narrows, hoping to cross into Laetia. The old boat took on water as soon as they shoved off. Those who were not rowing or paddling bailed the vessel or shoved pieces of fabric into the holes to keep it afloat. After three days the tiny boat slid onto the shore, the rotted wood giving way to the sand as it ran aground, close to the fortress.

"Soon, Baba Kerushk said, more pushed onto the shore, hundreds more, then thousands more. She explained how they used the wood from the wreckages to build crude structures to protect them from the battering winds and rain. The shelter grew into a village, then a town, then a city.

"As the city grew, so did the number of dead. The Nivs feared the dead. So instead of burying or burning the bodies, they left them in whatever structure they had died in and moved the living out. Half the city, by her estimation, was a necropolis.

"I told her that my men could remove the dead. That to help the living, the dead needed to be dealt with. She agreed, however reluctant she was. I met with Commandant Rayner and told him of what I had learned, this 'Darkness,' the fear of the dead, and the story of Baba Kerushk. The following day, I ordered five thousand soldiers to enter Carnum, retrieve the dead, and bring them to the pyres near the cliffs.

"The fires burned day and night for a span. Not just at Carnum, the light of cremation pyres could be seen at night from Lar and Fida. Forty-five thousand, two hundred and thirty-seven dead in the first purging of the three encampments. Not one male over the age of seven, only women and children. And every day hundreds more arrived on the shore. Some even said they had followed the macabre lighthouses from across the Narrows. Hundreds more floated in on the waves, claimed by Aequor in the voyage."

"Couldn't you have used the dragons?" I asked. "To search for boats in the Narrows, help rescue people out at sea."

Dem shook his head, "We tried. But even in a confined stretch of sea, trying to find a single vessel among the waves is impossible."

"We tried?" I repeated. "Did—did you ride a dragon, Dem?"

Dem's mouth pulled back into a wry smile. "Being a Commander has its perks."

My eyes grew larger than saucers. "Seraplaun!" I swore. "What was it like? Which one did you ride? Was it Balenax? I bet it was Balenax. Did you go over the water? What did he feel like? How—"

My interrogation was cut short as the door of the Sextant was kicked in. Five men in steel armor entered the common room. The soldiers scattered around the room jumped to their feet and pulled their weapons.

CHAPTER NINE

"We are looking for the Pirate Captain Gustavo Blanco," said the lead man, I recognized from the white plume on his helmet as Captain Wilhelm Striker of the Watch.

The room once again busted into laughter. My antics from earlier in the night had left an impression.

"Those aren't my men, Fer," Dem whispered to me.

"Aye, that's me," said one sailor near the front door. "Are ye wantin' to see me legendary cock?"

"Wanted for the murder of the daughter of a Lord of Drakkas Port," Captain Striker said. "And unless you're three feet tall, you, sir, are not who I am looking for."

"Aye, he's about three feet," said the drunkard. "Ye want to have a chat with the fella?"

The crowd burst out in cheers and laughter, bolstering the sailor.

On the other hand, I was sweating Iron Pins. Murder? An unsatisfied romp, perhaps. Stolen virginity, sure. But murder? No. I hadn't even punched someone. Everything I've done was completely consensual, encouraged even, by whoever I was with. Murder? No.

"Fer, leave," Dem said.

"I didn't—"

"Go. Now," Dem said, trying to keep his voice under the riotous laughter of the room.

I disappeared through the open back door into the night air. I ducked behind a stack of barrels in the alley behind the Rusted Sextant and waited for my eyes to adjust to the dark. A column of steel-clad guards blocked either end of the alley. I could hear more stomping on the stone sea wall in front of the Sextant. Half the Watch in Drakkas Port marched through the streets.

The Sextant backed up to the wall separating the docks from the Smuggler's Scourge, the slums of the city. Waiting until the guards on either side were distracted, I tried to time my movement to not be seen. I jumped on the barrels behind the pub and leaped, grabbed hold of the wall, and kicked up and over.

"There!" shouted one of the Watch, "Over the wall."

There was a flurry of clanking armor and heavy foot falls as some guards ran into the alley while others ran toward the nearest gap in the wall, several blocks away. I landed on the balls of my feet and rolled across the wooden roof of a hovel. I had made a point in my life of avoiding the Scourge at all costs. Travelers who wandered into the Scourge by mistake never made it out.

I figured my best chance was to run as fast as I could toward the Gate of Pane, where the monks would bring food to the poor, and try to push my way into the Temple District. If I could make it to the Temple of Res, god of justice, I could call for asylum, at least until I could figure out what was happening. Looking over the rooftops of the Scourge, I could see the large dome of the Temple of Res peering over the stone walls that separated the Temple District from the rest of the city. It was leagues of murderers, and thieves, and all manner of scoundrels that would kill you for an Iron Pin and the shoes you were wearing.

Half a dozen Watch gathered at the gap in the wall on the Docks side. Not even the Watch would enter Smuggler's Scourge in the middle of the night without reinforcements. I climbed off the roof of the hovel and into a dark alley. Peering around a corner, I could see no further than the edge of the building before the tangle of streets curved away.

Quiet as a drunken rat, I pushed south into the heart of the Scourge. With only a slight sliver of a single moon, the alleys and streets were full of shadows. I carefully slid from corner to corner, listening intently for the slightest sound. Getting to the edge of a makeshift building, I sprinted as hard as I could to get to the next corner and dropped into the shadows, hoping I was alone in the darkness.

Ten blocks from the Docks Wall, I paused and listened. Above my heartbeat there was a rhythmic thumping of metal on metal. The Watch had gathered enough men to enter the Scourge. I had seen the Watch enter Smuggler's Scourge a few times before, from a safe spot in the Market District. Standing three across shoulder-to-shoulder, and at least five deep, they would beat their swords against shields to announce their presence as they progressed. They would move slow in formation.

Step, Step, Clang.

Deep in the maze, it was hard to pinpoint where they were, but dozens of blocks away toward the east. The Watch was still far off, but they would insert units every dozen streets. I had to stay ahead of them, or they would intercept me before the Temple District walls.

I continued south, hurrying my pace while doing my best to avoid drawing attention to myself. I had made it a dozen blocks when I froze in my tracks. The sound of a heavy impact from the next street over. It was the unmistakable sound of someone getting beaten bloody, at least two or three against one. The Watch was just one problem. I could be attacked in the dark, run through and gutted for the handful of copper and silver coins in my purse. I could be pulled off the street by a "helpful citizen," and turned over to the Watch for reward or a ransom demanded from Zori.

The sounds of fists on flesh fell silent. I couldn't hear the Watch marching forward. There was silence in the Scourge as if all the denizens of the slums stopped and listened for my footsteps. The hairs on the back of my neck stood on end and a knot formed in my stomach. I held my breath.

Step, Step, Clang.

Step, Step, Clang.

Step, Step, Clang.

I exhaled hard, caught my breath and sprinted. Flying between alleyways, pushing past crates piled in the street. I cut through a small courtyard amid the hovels and turned a corner back into the darkness.

Step, Step, Clang.

Step, Step, Clang.

The Watch was closing the distance. As best as I could count, there were at least six phalanx of guardsmen that had entered the Scourge. It was more than I had ever heard used in a manhunt. And they were all looking for me. Why?

Step, Step, Clang.

I stopped to catch my breath near the center of the Scourge. I looked down a narrow alleyway. At the end of the row of shanty houses rose the prow of a ship vertically into the air. My eyes widened, and I could feel the blood in my veins run cold as ice. It was the *Kraken's Maw*, the home base of the Wharf

Rats, one of the most violent criminal syndicates in Drakkas Port.

Three-Fingered Fern, a pickpocket who stopped by the Sextant for a drink on slow nights, once told me about the Rats. He said he once got caught lifting a purse on Rats' territory. Three-Fingered said he was beaten to a mash and told if he ever tried to lift a purse in the Scourge again, the Watch would pull what was left of him from the harbor. Three-Fingered said they called their base the *Kraken's Maw*, because much like the real thing, anyone who saw it never lived to tell a soul.

And there it was.

The whiskey clawed its way back up my throat and my head spun. I slipped across the alley way and stumbled further south until I found a corner with good cover and a dark recess. I bent over, grabbed my knees, and vomited. My eyes watered and my throat felt like it was on fire.

Step, Step, Clang.

I looked out on to the street and seeing it clear, motioned to run, but my foot slid against the cobblestones. I looked down, hoping it was only the contents of my stomach. In the faint moonlight, I could see the thick, dark liquid I stepped in. I traced the path of the fluid with my eyes further into the crevice between buildings and found its source. I let out a gasp and then doubled over and retched.

Slumped against one building was a human man, young, maybe in his twenties. His eyes were open, and he stared straight at me. Three daggers stuck out of his chest and his throat slit. My heavy breathing became labored. My head spun. I closed my eyes to fight off the dizziness, but I could still see the young man's eyes staring at me. His mouth was agape as if to whisper "this could be you." I had never seen a corpse before.

Was he right? Was this the fate that awaited me? Could I hope to outrun the entire Watch? And even if I did, what then, would I hide in a temple for the next five hundred years?

I snapped out of my thoughts to the thunderous sound of the Watch a few blocks away.

Step, Step, Clang.

Step, Step, Clang.

Step, Step, Clang.

The Gates of Pane were only a few blocks away. I dug deep and ran as hard as I could, darting between the last few rows of houses on the northern most part of the Scourge. When I got within eyesight of the Gates, I ducked behind a cluster of crates at the end of the alley and looked out. The two large wrought iron gates stood fifty feet high with a golden horn-of-plenty on each gate. Just in front of the gate, two guards in shining steel armor stood watching for any movement from the Scourge.

I could wait for one to turn away from me. If I ran fast enough, I could tackle one guard and throw my dagger into the other. I could take out both and slide through the Gates of Pane into the Temple District to safety, covered in blood. No, that's not who I am. That would be a cold-blooded murder. I couldn't do that.

As I looked up and down the wall separating The Scourge from the Temple District, a hand grabbed my shoulder.

CHAPTER TEN

"Boy," a low raspy voice said behind me.

My heart froze. I was dead. The Watch had caught up with me. Or the Rats had found the reason for the disturbance in the Scourge. Either way, I was dead. I turned around, heart beating in my ears. The fire crawling up my throat. An old man, doubled over with age, was holding my shoulder.

"You hear 'em, boy?" the old man said. "S'not safe out there. C'mon."

The man motioned to the open door behind him. I tried to look past him, into the dark shadows of the room as he frantically motioned me inside. From the corner of my eye I caught the flicker of torchlight down the alley I left moments ago.

Step, Step, Clang.

The sound of the Watch thundered through the alley. The old man's jaw tensed as he moved to beckon me inside then slid into the darkness. I followed him.

Inside he placed a finger over his lips as the torchlight flicked under the closed door. I could hear the creak of the leather straps on the guards as they stood just outside. I dared not breathe. I couldn't blink for fear it would betray my location. My heart screamed in my ears. I was certain they could hear it. I stood silent for what felt like hours and stared at the old man with fear and the knowledge of my impending death in my eyes.

Step, Step, Clang.

They continued down the alley.

Step, Step, Clang.

I exhaled. I had never appreciated a breath of air so much. The old man and I stared at each other in silence for several minutes until the clatter of troops had moved a safe way down the road.

"Why would you help me when the Watch is after me?" I asked the old man.

"Weren't looking for you," he said. "They're looking for anybody. For someone to blame somethin' on. Scourge's a good place to find a body. Don't much matter if it's yours or not."

"I—I can't thank you enough," I said as I reached for my purse, my hands shook as my nerves processed just how close to death I was. The old man noted my intention and put his hand out to stop me.

"Ahmed."

"What?"

"Name's Ahmed. It's a sin to kill a man whose name you know. Besides, if you're headed into the temples, maybe you can say a word."

"I don't think they'll listen to—I'm not going to—"

"You got this far," he said with a smile. "Least one's watching."

Given my current state, the notion that anyone other than the Watch had their eye on me was insanity. I smiled a polite smile to Ahmed. By his reaction, he had seen that same smile before. It was one that had been used on me hundreds of times before in this city. It was a smile that both acknowledged and dismissed a person at the same time. And I had just used it on the man who saved my life.

"I should go," I said.

I reached out to shake Ahmed's hand. As the old man took my hand in his, I pressed the five silver palms I had secreted out of my purse and palmed into his hand. His eyes met mine with a mix of surprise and shame.

"By morning I'll be in a monastery, a prison, or dead, and they'll be of no use," I said. "I'll say a prayer for you whenever I get where I'm going, Ahmed. Thank you."

The old man did not say a word as I cracked open the door and peered out into the street, once again still.

"Thank you," I said again and slid out of the door into the darkness of the Scourge.

Shouts and commotion a dozen streets north told me the Watch had found a body. Like Ahmed had said, it didn't matter if it was mine or not.

I pushed toward the Central Market District.

The alley Ahmed's home was on spilled out into the Market's upper levels next to the Temple of Pecunia, the goddess of commerce and trade. As a young gnome, I had come with my mother during the feast of Pecunia to make offerings at the temple.

The temple was still as I approached it, dark except for a few embers in the braziers near the massive marble and gold statue of the goddess.

I rounded the corner of the temple to the front and I was struck by the emptiness of the space. The large golden columns of the temple were visible from anywhere in the Market. In the early morning light, as merchants set up their stalls, and the sun crested over the city walls, the temple would shine like a beacon. Sailors told me they could see it from leagues out to sea, a sign that with the new day would come riches.

From the steps of the temple I could see much of the market, much of the city below. The Market District was still at the late hour. The manhunt in

Smuggler's Scourge had drawn most of the Watch from throughout the city and the commotion had been a signal to the city to get off the streets.

I sat down on the cool marble steps to catch my breath. I had few choices left. I could try to make it across the city, past the Black Keep and through Gilded Hill to the Great Gate in the north of the city and out into the countryside. My brother, Dukhan, lived on the family's tobacco plantation. I could be safe there, perhaps for a while. But the Watch would come looking. Whatever this was, I didn't need to drag Duk into it. My only other option was to steal a vessel and escape by sea.

I laughed. *Pirate Captain Gustavo Blanco*. I was terrible at sailing, despite all my mother's efforts. The only ship I had ever helmed was the one Dem and I had tried to steal as kids before he joined the army. *The Esmerelda*.

She was a tiny sloop, one of the Southern Empire's ships used for quick runs to the nearby islands. Any two sailors worth their salt would have been able to handle her. Dem, an aspiring painter, and I, a student, were not sailors. Somehow, we had cut the moorings and partially set the jib, enough to get her moving away from the docks. Her voyage beyond the walls was not meant to be, however. Within a turn of leaving the docks, she careened into a larger vessel entering the Hydra's Mouth, crumpled *The Esmerelda's* hull, and she took on water. The other ship was dragged down and capsized. The whole mess blocked the Mouth.

When the Watch fished us out of the water, I identified myself as Captain Gustavo Blanco. Dem, to his credit, kept his mouth shut.

There was no way I could steal a ship on my own and try to sail it out of the city. I looked out at the harbor and the steady activity of the Docks, unbothered by the events in the Scourge. I remembered the *Delilah Fritzbink.* Captain Azpa was scheduled to get underway that night and with the arrival of the fleet, perhaps they were still there.

I stood and dusted myself off and made my way down the marble steps toward the Docks.

CHAPTER ELEVEN

*T*his was a stupid idea. I stood in an alley across from the Harbor Master's Tower. Despite the late hour, the docks were still a hive of activity. Stevedores hauled cargo from warehouses to ships. Crews hoisted barrels from the docks into the holds. Soldiers tottered from alehouse to alehouse. The cheaper whores loitered at the mouths of alleyways between buildings. The Watch stood within earshot of each other, on the lookout for the most wanted man in the Commonwealth — me.

From my perch in the shadows I looked over the crowded harbor and tried to find the *Delilah Fritzbink*. Sure enough, the small cog sat moored at the end of one pier near the Southern Empire Trading Company's warehouse. She was five piers over and a hell of a run in the open to reach the gangplank.

I studied the harbor. *Those ships are close enough. If I could get to the end of the pier nearest me, I might leap from ship to ship out to the Fritzbink.*

The timing had to be right. If the guards near the Harbor Master's Tower spotted me too soon they could raise an alarm and capture me. *Deep breaths. This would never work.*

A longshoreman carrying a barrel over his shoulder bumped into a drunken soldier who shoved him. The barrel clattered to the stone of the seawall, burst open and sent salted pork bellies tumbling onto the docks. The longshoreman brought a wide haymaker punch to the face of the drunken soldier, sending him tumbling ass-over-tea-kettle into the street.

Four guards on the docks near the Tower, and two I had not seen inside, moved to break up the fight. *This was my opportunity.*

I ran as hard as I could toward the end of the nearest pier. A large caravel with three masts was moored at the end of the dock. I ran up the gangplank and across the main deck and leapt straight off onto the carrack alongside it.

"Hey! You there!" a shout came from the quarterdeck of the carrack.

I didn't stop to look. I continued to run across the beam of the ship, placed one foot on the gunnel, leapt and fell ten feet to the main deck of a schooner moored on the second pier. My feet hit the deck and I ran up the gangplank and on to the second pier.

I had to run back toward the seawall to reach the gangplank of a massive galleon, the kind that would sail beyond the Narrows to ports on the far side of Laetia. I crested the galleon's gangplank and saw the Watch had taken notice of the commotion coming from the ships. I wasted no time on the galleon, grabbed a hanging sheet, and leaped to a carrack moored alongside.

I landed hard on the poop deck of the carrack and had to run down the ladders to find a point where I could jump to the next ship, a tiny sloop. I landed on the deck with a roll, then rushed up the gangplank to reach the third pier. Guards flooded on to the piers from the seawall and the nearby bars. A crowd gathered as well to watch the gnome dart from ship to ship.

And then I saw him.

The white plume of Captain Wilhelm Striker bobbed above the crowd as the Watch Captain charged toward me.

My lungs burned. My legs ached. I had to run. The nearest gangplank was fifty feet down the pier, a Southern Empire carrack. At the top of the gangplank I saw the Watch push past the sailors and the dockworkers toward me.

The beam on this ship was shorter than I expected. Where I expected to find a gunnel to step onto before jumping to the cog moored next to it, instead I found the open air. My back foot clipped the gunnel I had expected, and I tumbled to the main deck of the cog. Thankfully, I caught my weight with my face on the deck below.

There was a loud gasp from the shore. *Deep breath. There's a little blood, that will heal. I need to run.*

I heard the thunderous sound of the dozens of armored feet that clamored on the deck above.

"Find a rope!" one Watchman shouted.

I leapt to my feet and found a gangplank from the cog I was on to the carrack alongside. I ran up the plank and across the deck. As I became visible aboard the taller ship, a cheer rose from the crowds that continued to grow along the shore. *At least they got their money's worth.*

I rushed down the gangplank of the carrack onto the fourth pier. I could see the *Delilah Fritzbink* just a few ships over. I glanced down the pier. Twenty men charged down the dock toward me. The white plume of Captain Striker led the assault.

"Raise the gangplank and prepare to make sail!" Captain Azpa shouted. The *Fritzbink* was ready to depart.

"Aye, Captain." the crew responded and moved around the deck.

I ran down the dock. Several of the ships raised their gangplanks to prevent me from boarding. Near the end of the dock, I found a four-mast schooner with the plank down. I rushed onto the ship and darted forward toward the forecastle, jumped up onto the bowsprit and across onto the quarterdeck of the galleon wedge between other ships.

The mainsail of the *Fritzbink* fluttered as it was let out.

I ran aft, up the ladder on to the poop deck of the galleon and could see the *Fritzbink* below me glide away from the dock. I took a step backwards, ran as hard as I could, and leapt off the stern of the galleon into the open air.

I fell for an impossibly long time before my hands found purchase on the shroud of the *Delilah Fritzbink*, about halfway up the mast. There was a loud pop as my vision went suddenly white. I had dislocated my shoulder from the force of the fall. I screamed in pain and fumbled as I climbed down the shroud with only one arm to the deck below. I reached the deck and crumpled. Several of the crewmen drew blades.

Captain Azpa came to inspect the intruder on his ship.

"You had better have a damned good explanation for being late," he said in his thick Laetian accent.

"I swear I'll tell you everything once we're at sea," I said and grunted in pain.

"Gentlemen, it looks like my apprentice has finally arrived! Back to your posts, let us get underway," he shouted to the crew.

The single-mast ship silently glided away from the docks of Drakkas Port and toward the Hydra's Mouth as I held my shoulder and sat on the main deck. The massive walls loomed over the tiny ship. I looked back to see the crowd of armored men standing at the edge of the dock. A single white-plumed helmet soared out from the end of the dock into the water.

The *Delilah Fritzbink* slid between the two towers of the Hydra's Mouth and into the dark sea beyond.

All I had with me were the sweaty clothes on my back and a handful of small coins. My head spun from the pain, and the whiskey, and the run.

Perhaps in a month or two when we returned from Whyte Harbor things will have settled down, and I could figure out what was going on.

The world grew dark. I slid into unconsciousness. The last thing I heard was the Captain call for the midshipman to fetch the surgeon.

It was the last time I saw my home.

CHAPTER TWELVE

I t was well past midday when I awoke in the cabin of Tomas Flores, physician aboard the *Delilah Fritzbink*.

"You had quite an adventurous evening, friend," said the portly medic from the chair next to the bed. The doctor spoke with the same smooth Laetian accent as Captain Azpa. "Cort, fetch the Captain. Let him know our... guest is awake."

A young human boy with light oak skin and sandy hair rose from where he sat on the deck near the door. He scurried out without saying a word.

"I would imagine you are quite thirsty," Tomas said. He pulled a metal tankard from a shelf and half-filled it with water then handed it to me.

"Tell me, which hurts worse—your head from the thirst, your shoulder from the dislocation, or your pride from the fall?"

"Could I simply answer yes?" I sipped the water. The large man laughed as he returned to his chair beside my bed.

I recognized the sound of water crashing against the hull of the ship. "How far out are we?"

"A few hundred leagues from Drakkas Port," he said. "You have been out for fourteen hours, my friend."

The cabin door flew open. A man larger than the opening in a red tunic and sleeves of sailor's tattoos pushed his way inside.

"The boy said he is awake. Just who the hell are you, and what are you doing on my ship?" the large man's voice drummed in my skull. He kept one hand on a cutlass at his waist. "The punishment for stowing away is forty lashes."

"He is the son of Zori Alsahar," the smooth voice of Captain Azpa came from somewhere behind the looming hulk. "And more importantly, he is my apprentice. You will do well to remember that, Sergeant Leon."

The sergeant lowered his head like a dog just smacked on his snout. He stepped to the side to allow Captain Azpa to enter the crowded cabin.

"Reno, take Master Dufor topside. His parries are still weak," the Captain said, motioning to the behemoth and the young boy.

"Aye, Captain."

The large man slid out through the narrow cabin door. The young officer followed behind the brute, bouncing and eager for his training.

"I'll go get my cutlass from my cabin," the boy said down the narrow corridor from the medic's cabin.

The captain looked to the medic, "I trust we have the confidentiality of a physician, yes?"

The rotund doctor nodded to Claudio from his chair, then adjusted himself to face the captain and myself.

"I suspect you have a good reason for being on my ship," Captain Azpa said. Both men turned their attention toward me. "And one for why half of the City Watch was chasing you down the pier as we left."

"Because the other half was still looking for me in the Scourge," I said with a half-hearted smile.

The captain's eyes narrowed.

"Do you think this a joking matter? Boarding a ship underway without permission is piracy. I trust you are familiar with this, yes?" The captain did not raise his voice, but spoke with an intensity that commanded attention. "If you were the son of anyone else, you would take lashes from Sergeant Leon. The fact that you are resting comfortably in that bunk is because of the respect I have for your mother. Is that understood?"

"Y—yeah," I lowered my head.

"Excuse me?" the captain barked.

"Yes, sir," I said, my voice little more than a dry, painful whisper into my chest.

"Good," Claudio said. "So let us try this again, shall we? Why was the entirety of the Drakkan Watch hunting you through the city last night?"

"They said I had killed someone," I shook my head, "that Captain Gustavo Blanco had murdered the daughter of one of the Lords of Drakkas Port."

"Gustavo Blanco?"

"The sinking of *The Esmerelda*."

"Ah, yes. I remember that. Why did you give them such a foolish name?"

"Childish bravado," I shrugged.

The captain gave a nod of understanding. "Did they say which lord? Which daughter?"

"No," I shook my head. I looked the captain in his face, "I don't even know who the Lords of Drakkas Port are."

"No one does. That is the whole point. Only the Lord Regent, Alfons Silverford, is known," Captain Azpa said. "We all suspect the Lord of the Reach is handed down through Stormjaw line. But the others, the Lord of the Sea, the Lord of the Land, the Learned Lord, and the Lord Defender, those are anyone's guess. It has been that way since the Commonwealth was founded a hundred years ago."

"Great, so I'm accused of killing the daughter of the *marid*," I said.

"Oh, the Council of Lords is very real," Claudio said. "Though Silverford has no daughters. And you have had no interactions with Lusia Stormjaw, have you?"

"Not in three or four years," I said.

"Then, I must ask you an important question," he said. "Have you ever killed anyone, even accidentally?"

I looked the captain in the eye and answered with all the honesty I have ever mustered in my life, "I have killed no one."

Silence stretched for what seemed like a span as the captain considered what I told him.

"I believe you," he said.

"Well, that is a relief," Tomas sank back into his chair. "Honestly, murder?"

"There is still the matter of what to do with you," Captain Azpa said. "I have already told the officers and the men you are my apprentice. For the duration of our voyage to Whyte Harbor and back they will treat you as a midshipman, a junior officer of my staff. You will be quartered with the young Cort and join him for training. Unfortunately, we were not expecting you, so you will have to take a hammock."

"Yes, sir."

He turned to leave, then stopped as if he had remembered something. "I am well aware that you are some sort of minstrel at home. As a junior officer on my ship, there is to be no fraternization with the crew."

"No sir," I said. Two months and only able to speak with a handful of people. This would be a test of my will.

* * *

After another check of my vitals, Flores cleared me to return to duty. The doctor's instructions were welcome, given I had little interest in manual labor during this voyage. I was to avoid heavy lifting and take care not to strain my arm for the next several days, nor was I to climb the mast until cleared by the doctor. With that, he directed me down the corridor to the cabin of Midshipman Dufor.

When I speak of the cabins on the *Delilah Fritzbink*, you shouldn't confuse them with spacious officer quarters, complete with an ever-changing view of the Azurean Sea, such as you would find on the large galleons or pleasure schooners. Even for my size the quarters were cramped. The cabin Midshipman Dufor, Cort, and I were to share was narrow enough I could touch either bulkhead. There were no views of the outside, and the cabin was at the waterline. A single rack with a straw mattress, a stand for a wash basin, and a small wardrobe for uniforms were all the furnishings afforded to the space. Add to that, a gnome dangling from the overhead like a prized melon in a merchant's stall.

I had no possessions to speak of, save my torn shirt, breeches, and boots. As the rest of the crew were adult humans and an orc, the young midshipman and I were to share a wardrobe along with quarters.

As fortune would have it, a thirty-five-old gnome is surprisingly similar in size to a ten-year-old human.

After taking a mark or two to wash in the basin, I slipped into one of the boy's shirts and a dark blue tunic, doing my best to imitate the appearance I had seen so many times before.

I climbed the ladder to main deck just in time to watch a massive boot connect with the chest of my new cabin mate and send him tumbling to the deck. Two of the deckhands near the mast laughed as they tended to their duties and watched the display.

"A pirate will show you no mercy because you are small," Sergeant Leon said. He shared the same smooth Laetian accent as the captain and medic though he had a deep baritone voice that boomed across the deck. "You must be fierce. Get up, try again."

The hulking man saw me crest the ladder and turned his unwanted attention in my direction. I held my hands out, fingers spread far apart to show I had no weapon.

"Masters Dufor and Alsahar, please join me," Captain Azpa said from the quarterdeck.

Cort tucked his cutlass into a white sash around his waist and darted aft toward a ladder which led up to where the captain was standing. I bobbed and wobbled like a drunkard on a Carnis night bender as I tried to find my footing on the ever-shifting deck. The two deckhands at the mast roared with laughter as I swayed.

I reached the ladder and climbed up to the quarterdeck.

"You would rather he remembers us fondly when he is company paymaster," I heard Captain Azpa say to someone in hushed tones.

"Aye, Captain," was the reply, so defiant it was almost spit at him.

The captain was standing next to a dark-skinned woman with somewhat Elven features. He stared at me in stunned disbelief as I stumbled across the deck to stand next to Cort.

"You really have never been on a ship at sea," he said in a half question, half accusation. His tone made his intended meaning clear. *You are the son of a famed merchant sailor! Act like it.*

"No sir."

"Part of your responsibility will be to learn to helm the ship," Captain Azpa said. "It seems we may need to start with the basics. Master Alsahar, Lieutenant Adira Bitar, my first mate. I will leave you to her instruction in helmsmanship."

Captain Azpa headed down the ladder to his cabin at the stern of the main deck.

Lieutenant Bitar sighed, "Right, pay attention. Forward, Aft, Starboard, Larboard. Got it?"

Her hand pointed to the front, rear and either side of the ship.

"This is the tiller," she said with her hand resting on a long horizontal spar. She used a slow, antagonizing cadence in her explanations. "This is how you turn the ship. If you push the tiller larboard, the ship will move in that direction."

She pushed on the large wooden pole. The ship leaned to one side as it began a long, slow arc through the water. She then pulled the tiller the opposite direction, and the ship arced back.

"Now, you notice that even if you even stand on each other's shoulders, you cannot see beyond the forecastle," the first mate continued. "To navigate the ship, you need a spotter. Master Dufor, man the forecastle and guide us through an imagined reef."

The young boy darted down the ladder and across the main deck. He climbed the ladder up to the forecastle and waved back. Lieutenant Bitar motion for me to take the tiller. The massive pole rested level with my head. Bitar motioned to Cort across the ship.

"Shoal off the starboard bow!" Cort shouted.

Starboard, which direction was that? I tried to remember the direction Bitar had pointed.

"Make a decision, midshipman!" the first mate barked behind my head.

"Starboard, Right!" I pushed the tiller to the right.

"Congratulations!" she said. "You ran us aground."

"What? He said starboard," I said.

"He said the shoal was off the starboard bow," she spit the command back. "Again, Master Dufor!"

"Whale! Larboard Bow!" the voice was deeper than anything Cort could muster.

Bitar pushed the tiller the same direction I had a moment before. The ship creaked and groaned as it rolled to one side. I struggled to keep my footing as the *Fritzbink* traced a sharp arc in the dark blue waters. The ship leveled itself as a massive gray creature burst out of the water, curved and rose six, maybe ten, fathoms into the air before it crashed back into the sea. My knees buckled as water from the monster sprayed the ship.

"Sea monsters," I said in a tone so hushed no one could hear it above the constant wind.

"I think you've had enough for today," Lieutenant Bitar said as she noted my startled expression. "Master Dufor, a word!"

Cort scrambled from the forecastle and across to the quarterdeck.

"You were manning the spotter's post, were you not?" the first mate barked to the boy when he arrived, breathing heavy.

"Yes, ma'am."

"Then why did the call about the whale come from Mister Bly?"

"I was distracted by the creature, ma'am."

"Master Alsahar, you are dismissed," the first mate said. "Master Dufor, you will be scrubbing the deck from stem to stern. Perhaps that will help you focus on your ship and not a large fish."

"Aye, ma'am," the boy said, his eyes drifted down to the deck.

I moved down the ladder with caution, my legs less sure of each step as I moved across the main deck to the hatch that led below deck. I knew what a whale was. I had heard stories from sailors, read about them at the University. All the same, there was something spectacular and terrifying about seeing a beast three times the size of the ship breach the water only a few fathoms away.

The bracing, salty wind above deck stung my face and reddened my ears, even as the sun reached midday. The wool tunics of the officers made more sense now than they ever could in the hot, dry Drakkan sun. I climbed down the ladder into the dark interior of the ship. My nostrils were at once more assaulted with the odor of stale sweat and the tar that kept the old wooden boat dry.

I braced myself against the bulkheads and worked my way toward the cabin. My stomach, half-full of day-old whiskey and water, turned over as each wave crashed into the ship. At the end of the corridor, the door to Doctor Flores' cabin was ajar.

"Master Alsahar, a moment please," Tomas said from beyond the door.

"How did you know it was me?" I asked.

"I could hear you using the walls to navigate the corridor," he said. "You, my friend, would be the only one to do such a thing in calm seas."

I gave a sheepish grin and a nod of knowing. My innards were sloshed with every pitch and roll of the ship. My vision swirled and throat burned. Tomas recognized my condition and leapt to his feet far faster than I thought the large man capable.

He placed his open hand, palm toward me, against my stomach and muttered a few words to himself. I felt a wave of warm, soothing energy flow over me and then subside, my queasiness gone.

The doctor nodded with approval at his work then handed me a chunk of bread and sausage from the bureau with the metal water pitcher and tankards. He motioned me to sit in his chair. The leather padding embraced my aching body as I consumed the first morsels of food in almost a day.

"The sickness will go away in a few days," he said as he poured whiskey into one of tankards. "But that is partially why I called you in here,"

"Lunch?" I asked.

"No, no," he said. "Am I correct to assume you studied at the University for several years, yes? As I understand, it is the practice of the gnomes."

I nodded and swallowed a mouthful of bread.

"My father started my education when I was two or three," I said. "If you count that, I was a student for about thirty years."

"Thirty years! That is nearly half of my lifetime," he said. "In your studies, did you spend much time on the arcane arts?"

"Some," I said, unsure of his questions. "Mostly I focused on the School of Illusions, though I've dabbled in the other schools."

"I studied Biomancy, as you just saw," he said. "Have you had much practice in that?"

"Only a little," I admitted. "Enough to patch a minor scrape or cut. I could never tap into the *yili* of a person to manipulate the Fabric."

He nodded in understanding. "Finding a proper energy source can be quite difficult," he said, "particularly if the patient is severely injured. If I could show you how to draw the *yili*, would you like to study Biomancy while you are aboard? I could use the help—Lar knows Reno is of little use."

"Reno is an arcanist?"

"A battle mage," Tomas said. "Handy in a fight, but he is useless in the aftermath. I have heard the rumor the captain is too, but I have never seen it."

"Really? Well, if the captain agrees, I would be happy to help here," I said. "I'd be of better use here than I am on the quarterdeck, that's certain."

"Good," the doctor said with a smile. "I will have a talk with him this evening."

With that, I left the doctor's cabin and made my way back to my own.

CHAPTER THIRTEEN

I joined the senior members of the crew for supper in the officers' mess. A traditional Drakkan meal of goat stew with potatoes, onions, and peppers was served by the ship's steward. Fresh apples and bread were included on the table and a cask of ale brought from below deck.

The table was a fathom and a half long and made for utility rather than the luxury you would find on a larger vessel. It was crafted of the same rough-hewn timbers as the ship, with six simple chairs around it. Despite the lack of formalities, one could determine their place in the ship's hierarchy by where they sat at meals. Captain Azpa and Lieutenant Bitar sat at one end and discussed courses and current position. Tomas and Reno sat across from each other and debated which of the two did less work. Someone told me this was an argument that had raged for several years, each accusing the other of being the dead weight. Cort and I sat at the far end of the table. He was enthusiastic about having someone else aboard the ship to talk to. I got the feeling he spent a lot of time sitting alone at the foot of the table.

"Enjoy this while it lasts," Cort said.

I looked at him with confusion.

"The food," he said. "We stock up on fresh food when we are in port, but it's never enough for the whole voyage. We'll be dining on hardtack, bone broth, and dried meats once the fresh stores are gone."

"And we have enough of that to last the rest of the voyage, right?" I asked. "I'd heard stories of ships getting blown off course and running out of food."

"Oh yeah, that happens with some smaller companies," Cort said. "But the Southern Empire Trading Company always has enough stores for a voyage twice the length. That way we could get there and back without restocking if needed."

Pleased as I was to be here and not in a cell under the Black Keep, a week on bone broth and rock-stale bread wasn't what I hoped for.

"Don't worry, we also have fishing equipment," the boy continued. He ate as he spoke. "And Majid, Fawz, and Tamal are some of the best fishermen I've ever seen. Every voyage I've been on we had enough fish for the officers and crew. They really have an easy job on the ship. They spend a lot of time on deck fishing."

"You should try eating first, then speaking, my friend," Tomas leaned over and corrected the young boy. "It would make it easier for others to understand you."

"Yessir," Cort said as he wiped his face with a napkin.

"How many voyages have you been on?" I asked Cort.

"Fifteen. This makes sixteen," he said. "I became a midshipman when I was eight. My first few voyages were short, only a few days. But now I'm on the *Fritzbink* and gone for a span at a time. One day I hope to be an officer on one of the big galleons. I want to travel to Laetia, and Nivalis, and maybe even Jia!"

"Nobody's been to Jia in over a hundred years," I said. "I bet half the crew doesn't think it exists."

The boy fidgeted in his seat, "I know. That's why I want to go. How many voyages have you been on?"

"Successful? This one," I said.

Cort's eyes grew wide, "This is your first cruise?"

"The last ship I was on sank in the harbor," I admitted.

"You have to be a really bad captain to sink your ship in a harbor," Cort said with a chuckle.

"You do," I said with what I hoped was more amusement than shame in my voice.

After supper was over, I asked to speak with Captain Azpa and was waved toward the head of the table.

"I was hoping to skip tonight's astronomy and navigation lesson," I said.

"Is something the matter?" he asked.

"Between the chase and injury last night, and the seasickness today, I don't have much wind left in my sails," I said. It was a phrase my mother had used often when I was younger.

"If I let you go, I will not find you singing and playing cards with the crew in an hour?" he said. The captain had a way of asking questions that were commands.

"No, I gave you my word," I said. "Besides, I don't think I could lift an instrument let alone play it."

"Good," he said. "Then turn in early. Reveille is at dawn."

I thanked him and stepped out of the mess on the main deck.

I had heard several stories from sailors at the Rusted Sextant about what the sea did to a man at night. Not the creatures in the sea, those were stories cut from a different cloth.

No, the sea itself could drive a man mad at night. The vast unending darkness of the open sea, removed from the commotion of others, leaves plenty of room for a man's mind to stretch out and wander as it sees fit. Whales, serpents, even the

Kraken, the terrors of the deep do not come close to the horrors that lurk the minds of men.

I could not let my mind free to wander in the darkness of the ocean., not that first night. I needed it confined, sealed away. I needed to feel safe. Deep within the ship I kept my mind from the endless expanse of the darkness.

The sun erupted into an explosion of reds, oranges, and golds, the beautiful death throes of the day. I caught a waft of the lower decks mixed with the familiar aroma of goat stew I so recently ate. My stomach called for a mutiny.

I needed to brace myself against the bulkhead a few times as I made my way to my cabin and climb up into my hammock.

In the gentle sway of my makeshift rack, I found sleep with ease.

* * *

In my dreams, I returned to Drakkas Port. Not to the Sextant, nor my family home. Instead I walked the grounds of the University where I had spent so much of my earliest days.

Much of my education was at the hands of my father, the archmage of the Imperial University library. It was under his tutelage I first learned the arcane arts.

I dreamed of the Fabric, the many fine fibers of the universe that make up all that is, or was, or will be. The threads that tie all things together. With the threads of the Fabric, an arcanist can manipulate the world around him, bend it to his will.

In my waking hours, I sometimes thought I saw the threads of the Fabric. In my dream though, every thread was clear. I saw the threads of the light and the flames. The threads of people in the hallways reaching out from the distant past to the future. Some threads passed through me and changed. Other threads intertwined with mine and seemed to disappear.

I heard my father's instruction on the how to manipulate the Fabric.

"It is with this source of energy, the *yili*, that the arcanist can pass his will, his *agoti*, to the Fabric," he said. "Every magic known to man requires three components: energy, will, and focus. The *yili*, *agoti*, and *sebi*. With enough of these components I can pass my hand through a stone, create a fire in midair, or heal a wound."

"Where can I find the *yili*?" I asked.

"It is everywhere," my father said. "It is in the flames, in the sun, in the wind, it is inside a person."

Through the threads of my dream I saw the white glow of my father's *yili* inside him. It was strong and bright. It was almost solid. His *yili* held a certainty. I looked down at my chest. I saw the *yili* in myself. But where my father's *yili* was strong and certain, mine was chaotic, a constant state of change. One moment it was white, the next blue, then gold, green, red. It seemed like it wanted to take every form at once.

I saw a drill that my father once showed me to help train. I would stand in the library conjuring illusions of a ship sailing on the sea.

"Our *agoti* is only so strong," he said. "Every arcanist can only control the Fabric for so long before the *agoti* breaks. The process of using the arcane arts is draining on a person."

I would conjure the ship for hours. Sometimes it would sail past beautiful islands, others thrashed by the winds. Sometimes, the ship beset by creatures of the deep, would fight to stay afloat.

When I held my illusion, as real as the world around me, he had me stand nude in the library, to force me to maintain my focus. When I held my *sebi* while nude in a crowded room, he would have me juggle while maintaining my illusion, strengthening the *sebi* and the *agoti*. When I had mastered juggling five balls amid a raging tempest, he brought out a wire-thin birch branch and beat me with it.

The first time the switch broke my skin, my illusion collapsed. He would have me refocus and create the illusion again. Again he would strike me with the branch until he crossed my back with welts.

After I could control my *sebi* with the branch, he brought three of his apprentices. Each apprentice had a wooden training sword to swing at me while I maintained the illusion and juggled the five balls.

Every span he added another apprentice with a sword. After ten apprentices with wooded swords attacked and I could maintain my focus, he brought in the archmage of battle magic. Master Nami was a beast of a dwarven warrior, trained in a thousand ways to kill a person. Master Nami swung at me with a cat-o'-nine-tails as the apprentices stuck me with the wooden swords. My *sebi* was a rock. My *agoti* was iron. They bloodied my body but could not touch my mind.

I asked my father what it would take to meet his approval.

The ethereal gnome with silver-gray hair and sparkling blue eyes said, "My son, I've never trained an arcanist who juggled three balls and maintained an illusion."

I gathered my clothes, and too bruised and bloody to dress without the sting of a thousand wounds, walked naked from the library. I stepped through the large stone gates of the University and looked up to see the Black Keep in front of me. Then I collapsed.

* * *

"Sweet Mother!" I heard Cort say. It startled me awake. "The streets, you were—can you—create anything like that?"

"What are you talking about?" I asked.

"You had created a vision—a thing. It was a city street. I saw the black castle and the white castle."

"You saw that?"

"That was amazing!" Cort said. "I've never seen anything like it."

In my slumber I had cast an illusion of my dreams, filling the room with the shapes in my mind.

"It's not something I always do," I said. "I don't think I've ever done it before. I'm sorry."

After a moment I added, "could you do me a favor, not tell anyone I was casting illusions in my sleep. The other arcanists will not have the same reaction you did."

"Yeah sure," Cort said as he climbed into his rack. "Can you make anything appear?"

"If I know what it looks like," I said. "Otherwise I would just have to create something."

"Like a dragon?"

"I've seen those before."

"You have?"

"Sure, they fly over the city."

"I guess I haven't spent much time in the city."

"You'll see them some day."

"Hey, Ferrin?" Cort said, his voice slid toward slumber.

"Yeah."

"Why were you bleeding in your dream?"

"That's a long story."

I stared at the overhead as it swayed back and forth. After a few moments I heard Cort snore.

I didn't understand what the dream meant. I never trained like that. Sure, I practiced illusions, but the juggling, and the fighting? None of that ever happened. I never could control my *sebi* for longer than a few minutes. I had trouble pulling the *yili* from the proper sources; it was the reason I stuck with illusory magic. As for *agoti*? I think my time on the ship already proved how weak that trait was.

I lie in my hammock and swayed in time with the heaving ship. I wondered what would happen when we reached port. Captain Azpa believed me, but would the Watch? Would anyone else?

CHAPTER FOURTEEN

L ife aboard the ship was one of routine. The hammock I slept in helped improve my tolerance of the sway of the ship and after a full day of labor I found sleep easy. So when the crewman on duty overnight pounded on the cabin door in the morning to announce dawn I was not pleased.

The Captain expected both Cort and me to be in the officers' mess within a mark past reveille. It helped that young Cort didn't have a hair on his chin, so I could shave while he dressed. It was several days before I felt comfortable with a blade to my face while the *Fritzbink* pitched about.

Cort would leave to use the head while I cleaned and dressed. If I was lucky, I could scrape the previous day's stubble off, don the dark blue tunic of the company officer corps, and make it to the head before Sergeant Leon could unleash an unholy conjuration in the small, cramped space.

Once dressed, it was up the ladder and across the main deck to the large cabin that took up the whole of the stern main deck, composed of the officers' mess and the Captain's quarters. The officers used the opportunity to discuss the operations of the day, where we were along our course, and what tasks to do by the end of the day. Between the meal and the discussion, breakfast lasted a full turn. The slow pace of the morning breakfast allowed an added turn to get my bearings. I don't believe in my entire life I had ever awoken at dawn though I had heard passing tale of its existence.

After our morning meal and daily briefing, I spent two turns with Claudio as he tried to teach basic navigation to Cort and me. While I had a comfortable understanding of the charts and could plot a course with some competence, I soon discovered that I was useless beyond hope with a sextant.

At the third turn past dawn, Sergeant Leon worked with the junior officers on sword fighting.

That's an oversimplification of what happened. It's more correct to say Sergeant Leon batted us around like a bored cat does to a mouse he intended to devour.

Since I was half the size of anyone on the crew, weapon choices were straight forward for me. I couldn't even raise a cutlass, let alone swing one; that left me to use a small dagger for weapons training. With the smaller weapon, and almost no reach, I had to move to a perilous distance to fight Reno. Close enough, in fact, to allow the Master-at-Arms' large boot to connect with my chest and sent me sprawled on the deck. Each time either Cort or I would plant on the deck, Reno would let out his deep, menacing laugh. When he felt he had wiped the deck with the two small men, the Master-at-Arms called for Jabnit, the orcish deckhand, who worked with us on fighting stances and blade technique.

Midday meant a much-needed break for meals. The twelve members of the crew, save whoever had the watch, ate in the crew's galley below deck. The officers gathered in the mess on the main deck for a quick meal and an update of the day's tasks. As Cort promised, the early days of the voyage the meals included bread, fruits, and something that could pass as a stew or chowder. A tankard of ale was common at each meal. On occasion, a crewman would catch fish which they would add to the menu for both crew and officers alike.

After the meal, I reported to Lieutenant Bitar on the quarterdeck. While she gained no joy in my inability to determine directions, I think she enjoyed having someone join her for watch on the quarterdeck. After two or three days, I could tell larboard from starboard and bow from stern. As long as she was there to correct my constant mistakes, I was a competent sailor. Almost.

My watch on the quarterdeck was two turns under the midday sun. After that much time in the sun, a trip below deck to study Biomancy with Flores was a blissful reprieve.

A skilled healer on a ship the size of the *Delilah Fritzbink* was unheard of outside of the Southern Empire Trading Company. If I had to guess, I'd wager the doctor got a cut of the earnings at least equal to the Captain. But a crew with few injuries or illness was well worth the costs, according to my mother.

Burns, cuts, and food illness were common ailments aboard the ship. Cort told me that in rough seas and high winds a sailor could fall from the rigging and break his legs, and a snapped line could sever a limb. This time of year severe storms were an unheard-of occurrence in this part of the Azurean Sea.

Tomas tried to teach me the mechanics of Biomancy. The trick of life magic, as he explained it, was that you had to use the *yili* of the patient to manipulate the Fabric. He said the life energy of the patient was better for tending to wounds because there was a stronger connection with the body than an external source. He then spent a mark explaining how an external *yili*, if not controlled, could cause worse injuries. If a healer used an external energy source, the caster risked overpowering the spell, a mistake that could rip the patient's flesh from the bone.

Doctor Flores explained that if I focused, I could sense the *yili* of the person. He said it was like a ball of energy inside their chest. This was the *yili* the healer could tap into, the *yili* of the patient.

"This is all there is to healing," he said. "You find the patient's *yili*, and you remove their ailment, provided you have the correct spell to focus your *agoti*."

He handed me a large, leather-bound tome. On the cover was the word *Medela* and the outstretched hand within a circle, symbol of Carnum, the god of health and patron of healers.

"I expect you to study this during your time here and in the evenings," Tomas said.

Before I could protest, Fawz Khouri knocked on the door to the doctor's cabin. Fawz was an accomplished angler and ship's cook, Majid, often him assigned to catch the fish that extended our fresh stores. Embedded into meat of his right hand, just below the thumb, he had a large, barbed fishing hook.

The doctor bid him enter and offered him the chair. As Fawz took a seat, Flores motioned to tend to the crewman's wound.

"Remember to find his *yili*. Too much energy could rip his hand from his body," the doctor said as he took the book he had handed me and thumbed through to a wound closure incantation.

Fawz sat straight in the chair, eyes wide as a dinner plate.

"You know, I feel much better," Fawz said. He stood up to leave. "Thank you for your time."

I encouraged him to sit back down. As he did, I yanked the hook from his hand.

"Not anymore," he screamed.

I concentrated on Fawz's breathing, on the blood running down his hand. His *yili* surged bright and warm in his chest. It pulsed with each beat of his heart. I concentrated on the pulsing energy and set my *sebi* on his hand. With a quick look over to the tome Tomas had placed on the bed, I recited the incantation and willed the wound closed. Fawz breathed faster as the skin pulled together, the Fabric sealed his injury.

"Perhaps he will have a small scar," Tomas said. "But very good."

I did that. I willed his wound close and it closed. It was an immense rush.

The peace of Tomas' cabin was a welcome respite from the constant action of the crew on deck, the taunts and beatings Reno administered every morning and the hours in the sun.

Except for the few moments when asked to help tend to a wound, I sat quiet on a rum barrel in the corner of the cabin and read the *Medela*.

Three turns in the infirmary always seemed to pass faster than my watch on the quarterdeck. After my medical training, Tomas and I would climb the ladder to the main deck, the sky a mix of deep reds shifting to purples and blue, and head to the officers' mess for supper and another briefing.

After dinner, Cort and I joined Claudio on the quarterdeck for navigation by the stars. Back home in Drakkas Port, there was always some form of activity no matter the hour of the night. Ships arrived and departed, stevedores loaded and unloaded the ships, shepherds herded sheep through town from farms south of town to the harbor, and prostitutes and priests were busy with their trades.

The constant state of activity meant there were always arcane lamps, often known as mage lamps, burning throughout the city, casting a warm golden glow on the residents. In the middle of the Azurean Sea, the dim red deck lamps were the only light visible to the horizon.

Without the wash golden light from the city, a thousand stars joined the few I knew, more than I had ever seen before. For the first time in my life, I saw the night sky as it was, studded with countless stars and two fat, oblong moons, *Pateran* and *Matera*.

I wish I could tell you that as I stood on the quarterdeck of the *Delilah Fritzbink*, under the light of countless stars, I understood what it means to be a sailor, that I took up the astrolabe with a mastery unseen on the seas. But I was far worse with the astrolabe than I was with the sextant. And more than anything I wanted to perch next to the hearth at the Rusty Sextant and tell stories stolen from old sailors and flirt with merchants' daughters.

After two turns of trying to figure out which plates to use in the astrolabe, Captain Azpa dismissed Cort and I. After a day of honest work, the kind I tried to avoid at all costs in my life, I found the soothing sway of the hammock comforting and quickly fell asleep. The morning knock would soon start the process all over again.

CHAPTER FIFTEEN

In the dark of my cabin, I dreamed of home, my family's home. It was a palatial manor-house my mother gained after the collapse of the empire, where I was reared by a dwarven governess.

I dreamed of when I was a child, how I loved to sit on my father's lap in his study and listen to tales of the heroes in the Age of Legend. He would pull out his meerschaum pipe, carved into the shape of a dragon and toasted to a golden hue from decades of use.

Ignis would stuff the pipe with the tobacco Duk brought him from Merrywood. He would puff on the pipe as he thumbed through a tome looking for the right page as a thick cloud of sweet-smelling smoke circled his head. When he found his place, he would nod his head and say, "right then."

While my passion for adventure came from my mother, the stories I learned from my father fueled it. Father seemed to take pride in teaching. As with many children of five summers, teaching came in the form of stories with hidden lessons. Other children heard moral stories, like the dog that refused to help his friend and was scorned by the gods—a feeble attempt to instill obedience at a young age. Ignis read for me the histories of legendary heroes and their heroic deeds. I would sit in rapt silence as he told me about the orphan who killed a king, the many bloody wars of the dragon lords, and the slave that became a hero to his people. I loved the story of the young woman with the white hair, how she saved the gods and brought magic back to her people.

But my favorite story was the story of Pallum the Gnome.

Pallum was a farmer who was the son of a farmer in a small village on the southern side of what we now know as Greater Auster. This was long before they founded Drakkas Port, when Fortis was still a small fishing village.

After long days of toiling in the fields, Pallum would sit at the door of his hut and watch as the dragons returned from their hunting to their roosts in the Stormreach Mountains. He often thought about how wonderful it would be to fly great distances like the dragons, see beyond the farms and fields, across the sea, where they had to have gone.

One day, as he sat watching the dragons, he said to himself, "If I could catch one of those dragons, I could fly beyond the farmlands and the ocean and see where the dragons go when they fly away."

The next morning, Pallum filled a small sack with a fistful of nuts, three apples, a wedge of cheese, and half a loaf of bread and set off not to the fields but toward the mountains. He had no idea how far the mountains were from his home, or how long it would take him to get there, or even what he was to do once he got to wherever it was he headed.

He had known no one to have gone to the Stormreach and returned, no one foolish enough to attempt it. The mountains were towering peaks of craggy, red stone that reached from where the sun rose in the east to where it set in the west. On most days they could not see the tops of the mountains through the clouds. When they could, ice and snow capped the mountains.

Among the craggy, red cliffs lived a colony of red dragons. In the spring the dragons would fly down from their peaks and devour an entire flock of sheep in a pasture. Often the dragon would devour the shepherd. Shepherding was never a popular job in those times as a result, relegated to thieves and captured raiders.

The towering peaks that reached the sky and the gnome-eating beasts were not the worst part of the mountains. The Stormreach Mountains were also home to a fearsome warrior race of people known as the dwarves.

Dwarves are born to be combatants. It is said they leave their infants on a cliff face and only those strong enough to crawl their way back to the Enclave are raised to be warriors, the rest considered too weak for the tribe. As soon as the dwarven young are old enough to hold a stick, they train. Battlemasters then rank boys and girls, both expected to become warriors, based on their ability. At the top of the ranking was the king of the Enclave. Any dwarf that felt they had a better claim to a rank could challenge the occupant to a blood duel for the honor.

If the ferocity of the dwarves was ever questioned, suffice it to say the dragons found the gnomes in the valley far below a better prospect for a meal than the dwarves on the next cliff over.

Despite the dwarven warriors, and the cloud piercing cliffs, and the dragons' appetite for gnomes, Pallum set out for the mountains. After two spans of walking through fields and forests, past villages and farms, he arrived at the foot of the Stormreach Mountains. Looming above him, the red, craggy cliffs stretched up into the clouds.

While he stood at the base of the mountain, marveling at something so massive, a monstrous red dragon plunged through the clouds toward him before it arched up on the wind currents at the base of the mountain and soared off into the lowlands for prey. And so, faced with certain death, Pallum climbed the mountain.

Pallum climbed the red, craggy cliffs of the Stormreach, resting on ledges only a hand wide when he tired. As the sun set over the lush green plains, the clouds above him grew heavy and darkened. Searching his surroundings, high above the ground below, Pallum found a small cave in the cliff face. With a mighty push he lifted himself into the small cavern just as the rain pounded stone cliffs.

"Welcome my friend," a voice in the cave spoke. "You are late by several days."

"Forgive me," said Pallum. "I am not who you think. I was climbing the mountains when the storm struck. Your cave was nearby, and I sought shelter. When the storm passes, I will leave you in peace."

Pallum could see the voice came from an old woman with long gray hair. She wore rags, little more than a sack, like the one he carried with him, tied at the waist.

"Are you not Pallum, son of Kaylon?" asked the woman.

"I am," said Pallum.

"Are you not on a quest to see the edge of the world? To fly with the dragons?" asked the woman.

"I am," said Pallum. "But how do you know me?"

"You have been in my dreams for many nights," the woman said. "The Fabric of the World has shown you to me. I mean to warn you the path ahead is dangerous."

"And if you have seen what is to come, can you lend me aid?" said Pallum.

"I will give you shelter for the night," the woman said.

The offer relieved Pallum. He did not want to offend the hermitess. He thanked her and offered her the wedge of cheese he had carried from his home. He regaled the woman with tales of home and his quest to the mountains.

The rain fell all night, and Pallum slept well on the stone floor of the hermitess's cave. In the morning, the old woman presented him with three packages.

In the first package Pallum found food, a mountain goat slaughtered and salted and wrapped in burlap. The second package was a hempen rope tied into a tight coil. The third package contained a beautiful golden *kissar*.

"You are most generous, hermitess," said Pallum. "But I can not take this last gift. I am humble farmer on my way to a certain death. There is no way I can repay you for this kindness."

The old woman laughed.

"You left your farm months ago," said she. "Your fields are now overgrown with weeds. You left your own kind to climb a mountain no gnome has seen over. You faced down a dragon to climb into the home of a witch."

"You are a witch?" Pallum said, now scared for his life.

"I am what I am," the woman said. "I recognize what I am and can rejoice in it. You, however, do not see what you are."

"And what am I?" Pallum asked the witch.

"You left your home a farmer," said the old woman. "You return home a husband, a father, and a king."

The words of the old woman startled Pallum, but he took heart in the fact he would return home.

"But now it is time for you to leave," the woman said.

Pallum gathered up his belongings and the three packages, taking care to put everything in his sack. He bid the old woman farewell and left the cave to climb again.

Pallum climbed for days, sleeping in crevices to keep from falling from the cliffs. He thought about the words of the old woman while he climbed.

"How long will I be gone if I will be a father when I return?" said Pallum to himself. "It would have to be many summers before a child could travel any distance."

He put the thoughts out of his mind and continue onward. At last Pallum reached a massive plateau and a large cave high in the mountains. Mighty wyrms lounged in the sun as Pallum climbed on to the plateau. As you or I would regard an ant that was the dragon's response to Pallum. So small was the gnome he went unnoticed by the dragons as they basked in the summer sun.

And so it surprised the dragons when a voice thundered around them.

"I am Pallum. I have climbed the Stormreach and wish to fly to the ends of the world, to see what lies beyond mountains, beyond the sea."

The largest of the dragons was not lounging in the sun. No, the largest of the dragons was Tyrax, Queen of the Dragons. She was asleep deep inside the mountain when the tiny gnome began his thunderous proclamation. Disrupted from her slumber, the golden dragon — as big as a mountain —stepped out onto the plateau to see what had awakened her.

"You, tiny man, make demands in my home? I do not care what you wish," Tyrax said. "I wish to eat, and while you are but a morsel, I will eat you. And after I am done, I will fly to the end of the world and shit your bones in to the sea."

Tyrax brought her snout down, level with Pallum. Pallum reached into his bag and produced the first package. As he tossed the salted goat in front of the dragon's maw, the meat turned into an enormous pile of salted roasts. The Dragon Queen devoured goat and turned to Pallum.

"You are useful indeed, but that goat was far too salted," said Tyrax. She flapped her massive wings, about to take to the sky.

Pallum shouted to the dragon, "If you are to fly, allow me to go with you."

"Very well, but if you fall from my back, I can not help you," said Tyrax.

With that, the gnome climbed onto the back of the golden dragon. When he was in place, Pallum produced the coil of rope from his sack and threw it out. The rope, as though guided by some unseen hand, pulled itself around the neck of the Dragon

Queen and Pallum lashed himself to the back of the enormous serpent.

"What are you playing at gnome?" asked the Dragon Queen.

"I only wish to be safe during our journey," said Pallum. "You said if I fell you could not help me, so I only mean to keep from falling. I am not strong enough to harm you and have no intention to do so. I only fear for my safety."

"You are right to fear for your safety," said the Dragon Queen as she took to the sky. "It is I who intends to kill you."

The Dragon Queen raced through the sky at incredible speeds. She rolled, and spun, and slammed into the red cliffs. No matter what dragon tried, Pallum held tight to rope. When Tyrax had reached the edge of the land, she dove into the sea. Pallum held his breath as the serpent went deeper and deeper under the water.

When at last she could not hold her breath any longer, Tyrax returned to the surface. She looked over her shoulder and said, "Little man, are you still there, or have I rid myself of you?"

"I am still here," said Pallum.

"What can I do to rid myself of you for good?" asked Tyrax. "If I make you a deal, would you leave me in peace?"

"I want nothing but peace for your kind, Dragon Queen," said Pallum. "Speak your offer."

"If you want peace for the dragonkind, end the war between your kind and mine," said Tyrax.

"You are mistaken, Queen. There is no war between the gnomes and the dragons," Pallum said.

"You are not a dwarven warrior?" asked Tyrax.

"I am not," said Pallum. "And I did not know of a war between the dragons and the dwarves."

"For centuries it has raged. My clutch is the last on our island. I fear if the war does not end soon, they will banish the dragonkind to memory," said the Dragon Queen.

"Then I shall end the war," said Pallum. "You must do as I ask, but know I seek to help you."

"And what do you ask of me, gnome?" said Tyrax.

"Fly me to the Enclave of the dwarves, I shall end the war once and for all," Pallum said.

The Dragon Queen took to the sky once more, soaring above the clouds. No longer did she roll and spin, hoping to toss Pallum from her back. Tyrax the golden dragon flew to great fortification of the dwarves high in the mountains, close to the Dragons' Roost.

Tyrax landed on the mountain pass that led to the Enclave, and Pallum untied himself and climbed on the pass.

"Listen close," Pallum said. "When I call for you, come to my aid."

The Dragon Queen nodded and took to the sky. When she was out of sight, the gnome turned to the mighty stone fortress and walked up to the gates.

The Dwarves are renowned the world over for their poetry. It is said when the gifts were divided among men by the gods, they gave the elves arcana, the humans charm, the orcs strength, the gnomes wisdom, and to the dwarves they gave the arts.

And so it was when Pallum arrived at the gates of the Stormreach Enclave the dwarves greeted him with the poetic words that resounded through the ages.

"Fook off, cunt," said the dwarven guard. The other two guards at the gate roared in laughter. But Pallum did not laugh.

"I am Pallum, king of the dragons, lord of lowlands, and master of the sea," Pallum said. "I seek to challenge the king of the dwarves to a blood duel for the right to call myself king of the dwarves."

At this the guards stopped laughing. A challenge of a blood duel was a serious thing. And a challenge against the king, by an outsider no less, was an affront to the entire Enclave.

The guards called for their commander, who called for a minister, who called for the king. The king, Regus Stormjaw, intrigued by the challenge, bid the outsider enter. They led Pallum into the Enclave, a privilege afforded only a few, in that time or since. Inside the Enclave, they led Pallum into the center of the dueling ring in the center city. Word of the challenge against the king spread like a disease in a whorehouse and the stands around the dueling ring filled.

While the dwarves moved expectantly around in the stands, chattering about the outsider and his challenge, Pallum stood still. An attendant struck a massive stone bell, and silence consumed the Enclave. King Regus, the visage of a bronze statue to the god of war in his ornate armor and carrying a bronze axe as large as he, entered the ring. There were no cheers, no sounds, save for the crunch of sand under the king's feet as he strode into the center of the ring.

The king stopped ten paces from the gnome who still wore his simple burlap tunic and carried only his sack. Regus nodded to the gnome who returned the gesture.

"If you wish to have a second, I will call for mine," Pallum said to the King. It was common in blood duels for seconds to fight with the combatants, hoping to keep the honor of the family if one should fall.

The king turned to the archway he had walked through and shouted for his second, his brother Gresweld. A burly dwarf in ornate bronze armor wielding a spear and shield stepped into the ring.

Pallum turned toward the passageway he had entered through and bellowed a thunderous call, "Tyrax!"

The dwarven guards looked at each other in confusion, the gnome had entered the city alone.

Like a golden meteor, the Dragon Queen fell into the dueling ring. The force of the landing shattered the stones and shook the entire mountain. As the ground shook the great cylindrical stone bell that signaled the start of the duel struck the hammer and ringed out. Regus took a single step forward before Tyrax belched a jet of flame that consumed the dwarven king and his brother. The golden serpent bent low and grabbed both dwarves in her powerful maw, consuming both charred men whole. The entire duel was over before the dust had risen.

Pallum stepped forward and picked up the axe and spear of the slain king and his brother and held them aloft. By the law of the Enclave, the gnome was now king of the dwarves.

A dwarven cleric, dressed in red robes, stepped into the ring and bowed so low before Pallum his silver beard brushed the sand on the cracked stone of the ring. Before the cleric could speak a beautiful dwarven woman pushed aside him.

"I am Salia Stormjaw, daughter to the late king," the dwarven woman said.

Pallum nodded to Salia. He knew better than to apologize for defeating her father in an honorable duel. And as unorthodox as fighting with dragon may have been, so was fighting with a gnome. They considered the entire affair honorable by dwarven law.

"Hoping to retain some honor for my family, I ask to you to take me as one of your wives," said Salia.

Though humans, orcs, and gnomes each consider one wife enough for a marriage, the dwarves were more open in their relationships. High ranking dwarves, such as the king, could have many wives and saw no difference between men and women taking on the wifely duties. Regus, historians claimed, had thirty wives and would spend a night with a different one throughout the entire month.

Pallum looked to the cleric.

"All you would need to say, my king," said the cleric, "is 'it is so'."

"It is so," said Pallum.

"Then it is the tradition that a new king should go to the observatory at the peak of the Great Spire and look out over his kingdom," The cleric said. "As far as you can see shall be your domain."

And so the cleric led the new king, his new wife, his dragon companion, and the dwarven nobility through the Enclave to the base of the Great Spire. Pallum climbed the stone steps to a small platform at the top of the spire. He stood at the very peak of the Stormreach Mountains and looked out. The clouds, which gave the mountains their name, obscured the view so that no king had ever seen further than the walls of the Enclave.

Once more Pallum reached into his sack and pulled out a package, the golden *kissar*. The gnome held the *kissar* to his chest and then plucked the strings. With each note the surrounding air rippled with energy. With each wave the clouds moved further away from the Spire. It is said Pallum played the most beautiful song anyone had ever heard, and as he did, the clouds parted and the sun shone down on the Enclave.

As Pallum looked out over his domain, he could see the entire island of what would become known as Greater Auster, the island of Lesser Auster, the surrounding islands, and the sea. Pallum saw the ocean as far as the edge of the world. He called for the cleric who climbed to the top of the Spire and fell on his knees and wept when he saw the view. Pallum would rule over all of it.

Pallum climbed down from the Great Spire, to the crowd gathered below. As he stepped away from the crowds, Tyrax called him to her.

The Dragon Queen, with a careful claw, placed a small orb in Pallum's hand. It was an egg, a dragon egg, no bigger than a gnome's fist.

"I hope by giving you my child as your ward, you will continue to bring peace to our kinds, King of the Dwarves," said Tyrax.

Pallum bowed his head to the golden dragon, and she flew up into the sky. From that day forward, the dragons would entrust the brooding and hatching of their eggs to the gnomes, and in return the dragons would fight for the gnomes whenever they were called upon.

Pallum ruled over the island until his twelve hundred and thirty fifth summer. His reign was one of peace and prosperity for all the inhabitants of the island. Two summers after his death, a Fortean warship landed in a harbor on the northern coast of

the island. A thousand of Pallum's sons and
daughters and ten dragons met the warship. The
Fortean mapmaker assigned to the ship labeled the
inlet as the Harbor of Dragons. In their own tongue,
Drakkas Port.

CHAPTER SIXTEEN

For all the carefulness and caution Captain Azpa and the other officers used when working with me, afraid to insult the son of Zori Alsahar, Reno Leon returned with insults and aggression in our lessons.

By the fifth day of the voyage, I had enough of vicious taunts from Sergeant Leon. I completed the early morning navigation lessons with Captain Azpa and headed to the main deck for weapons training. As I reached the deck, dagger tucked into my sash, Reno came from behind the mast and swung at me with a wide haymaker that connected with my right cheek.

"The savages will not show you the mercy I have," he said. He drew a heavy cutlass and brought it down toward me. I pulled my dagger to parry his attack. He pulled the strike at the last moment. I moved to put some space between Cort and myself. Reno picked up a harpoon off the deck and hurled it at Cort, who twisted deftly to dodge the missile.

"Savages! Listen to you," I said. "What do you think we are? There are no savages in Whyte Harbor! We domesticated every island between here and a thousand leagues centuries ago."

He pulled the harpoon out of the deck where it had embedded beside Cort, turned, and hurled it at me. In a moment of panic, I did the only thing I could think of. I jumped over the side of the ship.

"Man overboard!" Cort shouted.

The crew in the rigging hurried to furl the sails as others scurried up from below deck and scanned the water for any sign of me. Reno stepped up to the gunnel and looked over the side. I clung to a tie-down just above the water line. As his barrel chest peered over the rail, I struck back.

I closed my eyes and tried to concentrate on the *yili*, the energy, and drew as much of it as I could into myself. With my *sebi* locked on the waves crashing against the hull of the *Fritzbink*, I made a fist with one hand and reached down toward the sea below. I muttered an incantation for water, the same I had used on the adventurer's armor a few days earlier.

With all the strength I could muster, I thrust my fist into the air. A massive wave heaved up over the rail and into the chest of Sergeant Leon. The force of the wave connected like a hammer striking steel and knocked him off his feet and onto the deck. The wave subsided, and I released the ocean from my arcane grasp.

My mind cleared, and I felt the hands of Cort and Jabnit, the orcish deckhand, grab me and pull me up onto the deck.

Several of the crew, relieved to see I had not fallen to my death, got a good laugh out of the sucker punch I landed on the burly Master-at-arms. Captain Azpa and Lieutenant Bitar glared at me.

"Master Alsahar, my quarters," the captain bellowed. "NOW!" He clenched his fist, his lips curled into a sneer as he pivoted on his heel and stormed through the door to the officers' mess.

Lieutenant Bitar smirked, "Congratulations, kid. That was an epic level fuck up."

Leaned against the mast, Sergeant Reno Leon held his swelling jaw and laughed deep and loud.

* * *

Captain Azpa's cabin made up the aft of the main deck. The dark interior lit with warm, amber mage lamps in large brass cages which swayed with the pitch of the ship. Ornate rugs from Aeromon covered the deck. Against the larboard bulkhead stood his bunk, a berth with a thick down mattress and adorned with silks. Next to his bunk was a sturdy oak chest filled with uniforms.

In the center of the cabin was a thick wooden table with legs carved to look like creatures of the deep. Charts, books, and navigational tools covered the table, and a single spindle chair sat across from the hatch, a thick oilskin coat draped over the back.

The captain stood, head hung over this desk as I entered his cabin.

I stood straight and silent, unsure of what he would say. The waves crashed against the hull. He beat his fist into the wooden table.

"You have put me into one hell of a position here," he said at last.

"He's been beating the hells out of me since we left port," I said. "I didn't think—"

"No, you did not. Did you?" He ran his hand over the company crest on the leather cover of a ledger.

"Not for one damned moment have you thought about anything. Have you? I instructed Reno to go hard on you during training, not to hold anything back."

"Why would you do that?" I gripped my hands to hide the tremor.

"Because piracy is real in these waters. Because they will kill me and the crew. Cort, he will he wish he was dead when they get through with him," he said as he turned to face me, his face contorted and deepened to a dark red. His eyes were glassy as if he was about tear up.

"You, you they will take and ransom. Or perhaps, if they are foolish, kill you to spite your mother. Your death would lead to hundreds of others. Zori would torch every harbor on the Azurean Sea."

I was so wrapped up in my escape, in what I would do when we encountered the Watch in Whyte Harbor, I had never considered an attack on the ship.

"And then you decided to be creative," Captain Azpa continued. "You used magic to attack Reno, in front of the whole damned crew."

"It was just a little water," I said. "He'll be fine."

"You do not get it, do you?" he said. "Use of magic to attack a crewmate is expressly forbidden. Anyone who breaks that rule is keelhauled. That's straight from Zori."

"Keelhauled," I said, almost a whisper. I read about the punishment once while I was a student at the University. Back in the old days it was a punishment reserved for the worst offenses. They lashed a line to a sailor's arm, run under the ship and lashed it to his other arm. They then threw the sailor over the side and pulled under and back up the other side. He'd be given just long enough to catch his breath, if he was lucky, before being tossed overboard again and again.

My stomach twisted. *That was my punishment?*

"Now, I think you see the position I am in," he said. "And every member of the crew knows it."

Captain Azpa let out a deep sigh and rapped his knuckles against the sturdy oak table.

"Even in combat training?" I said. "If I'm expected to train to fight for my life, one would expect a trained arcanist to use every skill at my disposal." I was grasping, but the alternative was too horrific to even consider.

Captain Azpa stood silent for a moment and considered the alternative. "You would still need to be punished for using magic unsafely."

"But not keelhauled?"

"No, but you are not going to like it," he said with a nod. "Come with me."

He pushed past me and through the hatch to the officers' mess and then out onto the main deck. I squinted as I emerged from the dark interior into the bright light on deck.

"Sergeant Leon," the captain shouted. "Ten lashes for Master Alsahar for the uncontrolled use of magic during advanced combat training. Tie him to the mast."

My faced dropped at the ruling. That brute was about to get ten good strikes against me.

Two of the crew, Bek Bly and Fawz Khouri, escorted me to the mast. Bek, a sailor I had met a few times at the Rusted Sextant, asked me to remove my tunic and shirt.

"Don't want to get any blood on it, Mate—err, Sir," Bek said.

I undressed to the waist and handed my clothes over. The two sailors bound my arms, waist, and feet to the mast.

"Here, bite down on this," Fawz said to me in Drakkan. He held out a block of wood, which I took between my teeth. "Gods with you, my friend."

By now the other members of the crew had made their way on to the deck to watch. Out of the corner of my vision I could see Tomas wringing his hands.

I took a deep breath and closed my eyes. The warm sun beat down on the deck, and I could feel the sweat bead up on my forehead and roll down my face. The ship rolled with the waves, back and forth on the choppy seas. The salt in the air burned my nostrils. I focused, tried to block out everything. My body shifted as the ship rocked.

The sergeant said something I couldn't hear above waves, then let loose his first blow.

CRACK.

I could feel the leather strips of the cat-o'-nine-tails rip across my bare back. Could feel my skin part and the sting rush through my body. I tried to focus harder. *Do not give this bastard the satisfaction!*

Images of the medical text Tomas had given me flooded my mind. Arcane charts, anatomical maps of the Fabric and thread lines rushed through my head. The waves crashed into the ship. I tried to remember the incantation for wound closure and recited it through the block in my teeth.

The whip came down again and again. I could hear muttered words among the crew, quiet at first then grew louder with each strike. I shut out the noise. Focused on the waves, on the sun, on the texts.

I felt a blow so strong my body shifted. But I didn't feel the pain. The next blow was even harder. The leather straps wrapped around my neck and face.

I focused on the waves. On the wind. On the sway of the ship. The strikes continued. Each time the blow would force me against the mast, against my bindings. Each time I blocked out the pain.

"Enough," the Captain shouted.

I inhaled sharp through my nose and opened my eyes. There was no noise except for the waves against the hull. The crew stared at me. I looked from face to face for some sign of what happened. Was I that badly beaten? I could feel the rush of pain wash over me like a pot of boiling oil and bit down hard on the wooden block.

"Cut him loose," Azpa said. Bek and Fawz rushed forward and cut the bindings. "Doctor Flores, take him below."

I felt someone lift me off my feet as my vision went black.

✳ ✳ ✳

I awoke in the bed in Flores's cabin. The bed linens against my skin burned, and I winced in pain.

"Well that was one for the books," the doctor said from his chair.

"How bad was it?"

"Devastating," he said. "Especially for Reno."

I looked over at him, my skin on fire with the movement. "What does that mean?"

"I trust you have been reading *Medela*," he said.

"Every night," I said. "What does that have to do with my beating?"

"I would expect anyone who received ten lashes, especially from Reno Leon to be a mangled mess by the time they got here. They cut you down without a drop of blood on you," he said.

I looked down, the white linens of Flores's bed were pristine. My dark brown arms were crossed with pale lines, fresh scars.

"I suspect you were healing your own wounds as your received them," he said. "How, I do not understand. The amount of *yili* needed to do that would be immense. As far as the crew, they think you are a demon, or perhaps a *djinn*."

"What about Reno?" I asked.

"You now have his attention," he said. "You will have to see if that means you have his respect. But, since you are uninjured, there is no need for you to be in my rack. Get up and study."

CHAPTER SEVENTEEN

I awoke the following morning to nausea and a searing pain in my back. The Biomancy allowed me to heal each wound as it opened, but it did nothing for the pain inflicted.

The netted hammock did nothing for the pain either. Thin lines digging into fresh wounds only made the discomfort worse. To his credit, young Cort had offered his rack to sleep in. But, unsure of how well I had mended my wounds, I feared I may bleed in the middle of the night and did not wish to ruin his linens.

As I lowered myself to the deck, I felt the bile rise in the back of my throat. I would face Reno in a mark in the mess.

I concentrated on the *yili* in my chest; it was brighter than before, stronger. Unsure of what that meant, I ignored it for the moment. I set my *sebi* on my stomach, just as the *Medela* instructs, and muttered an incantation to settle my queasiness.

"Are you doing magic again?" Cort asked.

"Just a little healing to help me feel better."

"Do you think you could show me sometime? How to feel better I mean," he said as he pulled his blue wool tunic over his head.

"Have you ever done it before? Magic?"

"No. Never. But I see you do it, and Reno, and Doctor Flores."

"Not everyone can," I said. "It takes years of study to attempt the simplest magic."

His eyes lowered to the deck, "I know."

"But," I said with a moment of hesitation, "we could try to practice some simple illusions." Cort's eyes widened, and a large grin wrapped around his face.

"Really?"

"Sure."

He finished fastening his boots and sprinted out of the cabin.

My stomach at ease, I headed to the wash basin in the corner of the cabin. I peered into the small metal mirror nailed to the wall. I saw the thin lines that wrapped around my neck. A single line extended to the jawline near my left ear. They would grow darker with time, an ever-present reminder. I pulled my dagger and scraped the black scruff from my chin, taking extra care around the new scars. I splashed water on my face and ran a comb through my dark hair.

I was procrastinating. Just the thought of pulling the thick wool tunic over the fresh scars on my back made me hurt. The rumble of my stomach snapped me out of my thoughts. Cort had brought a small amount of supper to our cabin last night, and if I didn't make it to the mess within a mark, I'd have to go without until midday.

I pulled the cotton shirt over the scars and tucked it into my pants before pulling the blue, wool tunic over top. I fastened my belt and dagger around my waist, leaving a little more room than usual to keep it from pressing against the wounds, then pulled on my boots.

I took a deep breath. The air was thick with the stench of a dozen men, the tar waterproofing, and salt of the sea. I opened the door of the cabin and made my way to the ladder and up onto the main deck.

Topside, I found everyone's attention drawn not toward me, but toward the horizon aft of the ship. Rising above the distant waves was the telltale silhouette of a massive dragon.

The ship glided along in the water, silent. The dragon, a dozen leagues away, floated without effort past us. It moved along our starboard side at what must have been an unbelievable pace. Within a few moments it was abeam with the *Fritzbink*. Within a few moments more, it glided over the horizon off our bow. For the first time, I understood the value the army had placed in those magnificent beasts.

"Messengers," Jabnit said once the serpent had flown beyond the horizon. "Not uncommon in Commonwealth waters to see them flying official missives between islands. If they ever figure out how to get a dragon to carry cargo, sailors will fill the streets of Drakkas Port begging for coin."

"That one's headed to Whyte Harbor?" I asked.

"Looks to be," he said with a nod and continued hoisting the mainsail.

I felt a chill run up my spine. Official dispatches between the islands, like information on a man accused of killing a family member of one of the most powerful people in the known world.

I hadn't considered that by the time I arrived in Whyte Harbor the Watch would already expect me there. Did they know the ship was headed for Whyte Harbor? Were they sending dragons in every direction? I supposed I would never know the answer to that. But I had to assume that anywhere I went in the Commonwealth, they would hunt me.

I looked off over the sea in the direction the serpent had flown. They would wait for me.

"They are a very good omen," Jabnit said as he tied off the line.

The mess was quiet as I entered. The notion of an officer scourged did not seem to sit well with the others.

I prepared a bowl of porridge and a cup of ale in silence. Gone were the fresh fruit and breads which were staples of each meal on the voyage.

The captain and lieutenant avoided so much as a glance in my direction as I sat at the far end of the table. Tomas gave me a sheepish smile. Reno gave a solemn nod but otherwise said nothing. Cort, used to being ignored at the end of the table, vibrated with excitement as I sat down.

"Did you see it?" he asked. "Did you see it? It was huge! It has to be a good sign. The sailors say seeing a dragon on your voyage is a sign of good fortune."

I stirred my porridge. "I've seen them before."

"He's on his way to Whyte Harbor," Cort said.

"Probably."

Cort continued, but I didn't hear him. I knew where that beast was going. What he wanted when he got there.

He wanted me.

The Dragon Riders, the most fearsome military unit in the known world. It was the force that laid waste to the Eisig Empire. The beasts that raised first the Fortean Empire, then the Drakkan Commonwealth, to dominance were hunting me. How does a single gnome stand a chance at finding the truth when the might of the Commonwealth is brought to bear on him?

I thought of my mother and father being brought to the Black Keep for questioning. They were respectable people. In the days after the Collapse they held the city together while other cities rioted and burned. I thought of soldiers and Watchmen arriving at Merrywood, the family farm. Weapons and armor gleaming in the hot Drakkan sun. I thought of them dragging my brother Dukhan from his home, in front of his wife and children. Would they march him back to the city? Would they throw him in an interrogation chamber, beat him until he told them where I was?

I looked up, the other officers cleared their bowls and returned them to the crate for the steward to gather and take below decks.

"Master Alsahar, my chambers?" the captain said.

"Yes, captain," I said as I took my bowl, still half-full of cold porridge, to the crate.

✳ ✳ ✳

"I trust you understand already the message the Dragon Rider was carrying to Whyte Harbor?" he said.

"Yes, sir," I said. I looked down at the thick rugs spread across the deck of the captain's chamber.

"We are fortunate," he said in his smooth Laetian accent. "Now we know they will be waiting. We have a span and a half to prepare."

He paced across the length of the cabin, reached the bulkhead, and turned back toward me. "So, what is your plan?"

"I—I don't have one."

He nodded as though he expected as much.

"I have made the importance of your combat training clear to you, yes?"

"Yes, sir, you have," I said. I ran an absent-minded hand over the fresh scars on my arms.

"The road you are going down, it will be important that you can defend yourself," he said.

"Against dragons?!"

"They will not attack you with dragons," he said with an incredulous air. "They want you alive. You are no good to them burned to a crisp. So you must defend yourself against men."

"How do I do that?"

"To start, no more navigation or training at the helm. You will train with Reno the entire morning," he said.

I scoffed, but he paid no attention to my protest.

"You will stand watch in the infirmary with Doctor Flores, I suspect his training is more effective than you currently realize," he continued. "After supper, you will spend another four hours with Reno and anyone he sees fit to include. I expect you to be an able swordsman when you step off this ship. Reno and I will also work with you on battle magic. Have you ever studied arcane combat?"

"I read a few books at the University," I said. "I could never seem to wrap my head around it."

"It is not a simple skill to read and learn," he said. "Perhaps that is for the best. Drakkas Port would have been destroyed a thousand times over by curious magelings if it could."

135

"Does Reno know why he is teaching me these things?"

"Beyond what I have already told him, no," Captain Azpa said. He looked me in the eye. "That is not my story to tell."

CHAPTER EIGHTEEN

The sun was blinding as I stepped through the hatch from the officers' mess onto the main deck. One hand was on my dagger as I expected Reno to take advantage of the glare to attack.

As my eyes adjusted to the bright light, I saw the hulking man stood along the larboard rail. He watched the waves crash against the hull of the *Delilah Fritzbink*. A board in the deck groaned under my foot. He turned, saw me, and motioned to join him.

"Do you know the secret to unlimited *yili*?" His voice almost inaudible over the sound of the water. The question was more philosophical than I expected from the brute.

"There is no such thing," I responded. "*Yili* is energy. It is everywhere, but a mage cannot create it, only transfer it from one thread to another. A mage that tries to control the *yili* will drive himself mad." The rote response of decades of arcane training poured out of me.

He nodded but did not take his eyes from the water. "That is good to remember. The *yili* in a man is not enough to drive a biomancer insane. Nor is the *yili* of a fireplace or bonfire enough to consume an illusionist," he said. "But can you imagine the *yili* found in the entire sea?"

Just considering that amount of energy was enough to make my head hurt. Based on my studies with Tomas, the amount of *yili* required to mend a wound was less than that required for a single heartbeat. I looked out at the waves rolling in the open water, and I considered Reno's question.

"Can you imagine the *yili* of a thousand men in battle? Ten thousand men?" he continued. "With that much power, what could you do?"

"Anything," I said before my mind processed the question he had asked.

"And yet there it is, for you to take," Reno said making a grand sweep of the Azurean Sea. "What would you do with it?"

"Is that where battle mages get the *yili*?" I asked.

He closed his eyes and traced a sign in the air with his right hand.

"Fireball off the larboard side!" he thundered.

The crew on deck spun toward the larboard side as an orb of flame five fathoms across erupted from thin air over the open water. The force of the blast sent a hot breeze back toward us, caused the sails to flutter before they snapped taut once again.

From the forecastle of the ship Blake Bly let out a maniacal howl. "Thanks for the warning!"

"How?" It was all I could utter.

"You have felt it already," Reno said. "Just yesterday, I am certain. Once you have tapped into the source of the *yili* available, it is a simple matter of *agoti*."

"Oh, a simple matter of *agoti*," I said. "I will a giant ball of fire to exist, and there it is."

"You can will an image from the ether, can you not?" he responded. "You will sound amongst the crowd during your shows. Just yesterday you willed the waves to rise from the sea and strike me. Why do you now believe a flame is any different?"

My eyes searched out over the waves.

"*Sebi. Yili. Agoti*," he said. "Focus, energy, will. That is all there is to it."

"And the hand gesture?" I asked.

"You shouted the arcane word for water, and the water rose. I traced the alchemical symbol for fire, and the fire came. Each caster has his own method for projecting his *agoti*," the brute said. "Now, create a fire over the waves."

I closed my eyes. The ship rocked back and forth on the waves. My *sebi* set. The energy swirled all around me. The sun, the waves, the men on the ship. The sense of the waves crashed over me, the deep churn of the sea filled my mind. I felt the *yili* of the waves build. *I'll show Reno how strong of a mage I am.*

I shouted the invocation for fire and thrust my hand out toward the horizon and opened my eyes.

Nothing.

"You released your *sebi* too soon," he said. "You wanted to show off."

"How could you know that?"

"You smirked just before you released the invocation," he said. "Do it again!"

I huffed and adjusted my shoulders. I was a trained arcanist with decades of study in the University and I was being showed up by a tattooed gorilla.

"*Sebi. Yili. Agoti*," he shouted.

I closed my eyes and focused once again on the waves. The *yili* filled my mind just as quick as it had before. I raised my hand. My whole mind went white as the force of a massive palm struck me on the back of my head and nearly sent me over the rail.

A roar of laughter came from Reno, "You must block out everything. Your life, the lives of your men depend on your ability to cast that spell. Again!"

I sneered and adjusted my neck. The back of my head still stung from the last strike.

"*Sebi. Yili. Agoti*," the massive man shouted.

I was reluctant to close my eyes again. I tried to set my *sebi* with my eyes open, but just couldn't do it. I closed my lids and focused on the arcane Fabric. The sense of the *yili* around me was comforting. Without opening my eyes, I thrust my hand out to the horizon and shouted the invocation for fire in a guttural yell. I sensed the energy of the sea flow through me into the sky at the point I selected.

As I opened my eyes, I could see a small flame flickering on the horizon, the ball of fire no larger than a cooking fire. A loud pop reverberated over the water as the Fabric released the excess energy. My father called them the Novice's Thrum, a spell with too much *yili* pushed through a thread. It was a clear sign of how inefficient the spell was.

"Good," Reno said. "I expect you to do that anytime I command it, understood?"

I nodded.

"Jabnit! Let us raise the stakes," the brute said as he pulled his cutlass from his waist.

The orc, leaned against the mast, pulled his own cutlass and a dagger, and approached.

In the days I had been on board the *Delilah Fritzbink* I had grown accustomed to rounds of combat with Jabnit and even occasionally Reno, but never had I tried to fight both at the same time.

It's just like drunks at the Sextant. Breathe and dodge.

Reno's heavy cutlass arced wide on my left side. I twisted and allowed the blade to crash into the deck. Jabnit had closed the distance faster than I had expected and was close enough to swing his cutlass toward my midsection. The height difference made it easy to use my dagger to deflect the blade into the deck.

"Fireball, starboard side!" Reno shouted.

I extended my arm and launched a pathetic flame that flickered over the open water, then turned back to see Jabnit's dagger race toward me. I spun on the ball of my foot and used the orc's momentum to pull him off balance and across the deck.

"*Sebi. Yili. Agoti*," the battle mage shouted. "Fireball, larboard side!"

I focused on the flame, but the flat of Reno's sword struck my arm as I attempted the invocation.

"*Sebi! Yili! Agoti!*"

Jabnit feigned a low strike with his cutlass and brought his dagger across the front of my chest. I rocked backwards, but the sharp blade found purchase in my tunic and cut a small gash across my chest.

"Master Dufor, I believe it's time for your combat lessons!" Reno shouted up to the quarterdeck then extended his massive boot into my chest.

Still off balance from Jabnit's attack, the boot connected and sent me sprawled to the deck near the ladder to the quarterdeck. I looked up and saw the Cort, blade drawn, leap from the ladder to strike down at me. I rolled, and his cutlass crashed into the deck.

"Water Column, starboard side!" Reno shouted.

I anticipated the next command, but the call for water caught me by surprise. I let a flame go over the waves. It sputtered and collapsed in an instant. "Dammit," I said.

"That does not look like water, Master Alsahar," Reno shouted. "There is water all around us if you need a reminder."

He had taken up a position near the forecastle, with Jabnit on the starboard side and Cort on the larboard.

Jabnit slashed at me with his cutlass, high and wide, as Cort followed with a low thrust to my midsection.

I stepped closer to Jabnit, inside his reach and struck him in the thigh with my open hand as I deflected Cort's blade with my dagger.

"Fireball, starboard! Water Column, larboard!" Reno shouted.

I released a ball of flame no larger than my fist and used the motion of summoning the water column to connect a punch across Jabnit's chin. The fist connected but managed little more than a strong wave.

Jabnit reeled backward from the unexpected punch, and Reno took a step forward and hurled a harpoon at me. I stepped left and shoved Cort as hard as I could.

I shouted the invocation for wind and thrust both hands forward. A breeze caught the sails, enough to heave the ship forward and throw both Reno and Jabnit off balance.

"Good!" Reno shouted as he regained his footing. "Use the environment to your advantage."

Cort found his balance as the ship swayed and pressed me with a series of wild swings which forced me to retreat.

"Pull your *yili* from the surrounding commotion," Reno shouted.

I adjusted my *sebi*, pulled the *yili* from the energy of the battle, and gasped. It was as though Cort and Jabnit moved at a fraction of the speed they had been fighting. I found their attacks sluggish, easier to deflect, and could even find opportunities to riposte Jabnit.

"Fireball, starboard side!" Reno shouted.

I released the *yili* over the starboard side in a fist-sized ball of flame and another Thrum.

My attackers used the sudden release of energy to attack with renewed speed. Jabnit rushed forward and landed a strong right cross to my chin that sent me backwards. Cort lashed out with his blade. He managed a strike or two before they slowed again.

"Lightning, larboard side!" the brute bellowed.

Lightning? I don't even know the right word to call. I used the arcane word for spark and brought my fist down to the deck as a flicker of purplish energy crackled against the water only a fathom from the rails. An observer would be hard-pressed to call it lightning, but the Thrum was deafening.

The two combatants rushed forward. I parried a strike from Cort and dodged an offhand blow from

Jabnit. I rolled underneath the ladder to the quarterdeck as the two attackers slowed again.

I focused on the motion of the ship, on the movement of my sparring partners.

From the stern of the ship came a thunderous roar and beating of massive leathery wings. An enormous red dragon hovered over the stern of the ship.

"Dragon astern!" Bly shouted from the forecastle.

"No shit!" Lieutenant Bitar said as she threw the tiller to one side. The *Delilah Fritzbink* listed hard as the ship tacked starboard to escape the dragon.

Jabnit and Cort dropped their weapons to the deck, their eyes transfixed on the serpent.

The dragon lowered its head, level with the ship and snorted a puff of air that stunk of sulfur and burning cinders.

Reno stood full upright and applauded. "Enough!" he bellowed. And just as at it had appeared, the dragon was no more.

I stepped out from underneath the ladder and Reno clapped me on the back and laughed.

"The sulfur scent was a nice touch, but dragons don't smell like cinder close up," he said.

"What the fuck!" Bitar shouted from the quarterdeck.

"Just an illusion," Reno replied. "A damned good one too."

CHAPTER NINETEEN

Each day we drew closer to Whyte Harbor.
Each day I grew somewhat more confident in
my abilities to defend myself. It became a
routine. Wake up, wash, eat, fight.

I would tend to any wounds on the ship, most
often my own, for a few turns. After my rounds, I
got an evening meal, followed by more fighting. We
battled until the glow of fireballs exploding over the
water was the only light we could see.

Parries and ripostes filled my dreams. Day after
day, eight turns of combat training as the *Delilah
Fritzbink* glided toward the inevitable. Toward my
fears. Toward the unknown.

I can never repay Reno and Captain Azpa for
keeping my mind occupied during those days. There

wasn't enough time to fret over what would happen when I got to Whyte Harbor. I had to stay focused for the next attack that could come at any moment.

Jabnit proved to be a deep well of wisdom on the art of the blade. I soon learned foundational positions of the Orcish War Dance, a series of movements intended to teach young orcs how to use a blade in combat.

By the third day of intensive training I was as comfortable with a blade in my hand as Cort. Much of my confidence in combat came from years of dodging fists in Dockside. Soon, Reno encouraged other members of the crew to fight one-on-one or in pairs, all under his watchful eyes.

First was sailmaker Kane Cloud, a burly Aeromonian who smelled like he had just a crawled out of a tobacco jar. His swings were wide, uncontrolled, and allowed me to climb easily inside his reach and land attacks with my dagger, a move Jabnit called Burrowing Rabbit.

After the sailmaker came the carpenters, Suud Amari, the dark-skinned Drakkan, and the one-eyed Elazaro Wion. Suud preferred dual daggers while Elazaro opted for a rapier. Suud tried his best to circle behind me while the cyclops tried to dazzle me with flourishes and motions Jabnit described as useless dancing.

If his flourishes provided any tell, it made it clear Elazaro had never battled a gnome before. Each of his ornate strikes ended two hands above my head before he returned to his starting position with a swish of the thin blade.

"Movement," Jabnit explained, "should be deliberate. You should conserve your energy, your body ready to react, to strike."

As Elazaro twirled into me with a fresh series of strikes, I stepped to my left and pulled the *yili* from his blade. The well of energy grew inside me and the blade slowed. With a deliberate step I closed the distance between us, set my *sebi* and thrust my heel into the instep of his foot and shouted the arcane word for rock. It was my own take on the Angered Mule position. The sound of bones snapping reverberated on the deck followed by the screams of Elazaro as he fell.

I pulled back to a defensive stance, Greedy Goblin, but as I set my feet, I felt the sting of steel rip across my back. Suud found an opportunity while I was distracted and struck. The Drakkan pushed through the blow to knock me off my feet. As I tumbled, I felt the second dagger slide between my lower ribs.

I opened my mouth to scream but could only taste blood. I tried to gather the *yili*, to set my *sebi* to seal the wound. As my knees hit the deck, I felt cold. Darkness consumed my vision. Somewhere in the distance I heard shouts. Someone called for the surgeon.

* * *

"When I said I would see you after the midday meal," Tomas said, "I did not mean as a patient."

Once again, I woke in the doctor's bed. The round, red-faced medic stood over the console and poured himself a glass of a whiskey. On the floor next to me lay Elazaro, unconscious, his foot wrapped in a splint.

"Is he well?" I asked, my head still spinning.

"Physician, heal yourself," Tomas said with a chuckle as he sipped his drink. "He will be fine, though you broke his foot in four places. It took a turn to set the bones. And that was after I closed you up."

He collapsed in the chair next to bed with a huff. "You may have a *yili* as endless as the sea," he waved his drink for emphasis, "but I am spent."

Within a moment the heavy breath from the chair became a snore.

I reached down and touched the bare side of my chest. There was a raised scar, about the size of my thumb, between my ribs on my lower left side. A few ribs higher and Suud would have undoubtedly received a medal from the Watch: *For Service to the Commonwealth.*

The waves crashed against the hull. I concentrated on the water, the rocking of the ship, found the *yili*, and pulled it inside. With the warmth of light inside my chest, I set my *sebi* on Elazaro and began the incantation to fuse the broken bones. There was a sickly pop as a fracture Tomas had missed moved into place. Elazaro shot up on his bedroll with a piercing scream.

Tomas, shaken from his slumber, looked around confused. Elazaro was panting, wide-eyed from the pain.

"I—I set the foot," I said. "There was a missed fracture. I was trying to help fuse the bones, perhaps get him walking again. I didn't expect there to be an unset fracture."

Tomas walked around to where the carpenter sat next to the bed and knelt to examine the foot. Elazaro winced in pain. The doctor prodded and ran a firm finger down the instep.

"I will be damned," Tomas said. "I will be damned. Well, it looks like you will be walking again in no time, Zaro!"

The doctor turned to me, "And if you are well enough to heal others, you are well enough to recover in your own cabin."

"So, I can go?" the carpenter asked.

"You can," the doctor said. "Cort!"

The hatch opened, and the shaggy haired boy stuck his head into the cabin.

"Get a few men and have them help Mister Wion to his bunk," the doctor said. "And then come claim your cabinmate."

"Yessir," the boy said and darted from the room. A moment later he was back and helped me to my feet.

As we stepped into the passageway, my right arm slung over his shoulder for support, he said "You can sleep in my rack tonight. You'll tear your wounds open again if you climb up there."

I nodded, too weak to argue with him.

"By the way, that's four."

"Four what?"

"Shirts. That's the fourth shirt of mine you've slashed and bled on. You know it'll be colder in Whyte Harbor. I'd like to have a few when we get there."

"Cort," I said as I pulled my legs onto the soft hay mattress and lay back, "When this is all over, I'll buy you a dozen shirts and the nicest boots in Drakkas Port."

"If you insist," he said and climbed into the hammock.

CHAPTER TWENTY

O n the sixteenth day of the voyage, I awoke in my hammock to the rhythmic swaying of choppy seas. In his usual fashion, Cort dressed and headed to the main deck before my feet touched the timbers of our cabin deck. I washed my face and noticed the stubble was filling into a full beard.

I had given up shaving in the mornings a few days after the whipping. In part it was to let the wounds on my neck heal, but I thought it a small form of rebellion. They could have their uniforms and regimented days. I would have a beard.

After a span of growth, the short black scruff and my brown skin made me look older, like a sailor, like the old salts that often floated into the Rusted Sextant with the tide. I wasn't the only crew member with a beard. Bly and Elazaro both wore full beards, and Captain Azpa had a neatly trimmed goatee. But this was my rebellion, worn openly, flaunted.

Blessings to Lar, I had figured out a way to wash my only pair of pants. I lathered them with a lye soap, tied them at the leg with a line, and cast them overboard. By the end of the first span they smelled worse than the lower decks. I also was more careful of damaging Cort's shirts. Though in a three-on-one spar with Reno, Jabnit, and Suud, I lost another when Reno caught my shirt with the tip of his cutlass and tore it from my body. Cort had fifteen shirts when he left Drakkas Port. Now he was down to ten. At the rate I was going, we would both be reporting for training bare chested soon.

I didn't bother with the wool tunic that morning. Reno would have me take it off in a few marks anyway when we trained. I opened the hatch to our cabin and startled Tomas as he was leaving his own.

"Ah, Ferrin, try to go easy with the weapons today. I have a feeling I will have need of your talents this evening," he said.

"My talents? Why is that?" I asked.

"Heavy seas," he said and pushed his way down the corridor to the ladder. "Storm is brewing."

I followed the doctor up the ladder to the main deck. The early morning sky was a deep, brilliant red. The crew busied themselves with getting sails set and clearing the deck of anything not secured. I glimpsed Jabnit in the rigging. He fidgeted the way he did before our fights. Tension. Anxiety. Whatever he expected, he didn't think it would be good.

Tomas and I crossed the deck and entered the officers' mess. Reno stood in at the table briefing the others when we walked in.

"The men are panicked over the storm," the hulking man said, "claim they have seen nothing like it in the Azurean."

"It's just a storm," Bitar said. "Everything'll be peaceful by evening."

"All the same, the men would like to make an offering to Aequor," Reno said, "if the Captain will allow it."

Bitar scoffed, "It's a waste of good wine."

Reno looked like he was about to reply when Captain Azpa raised his hand to interject. "If a barrel of wine will put the crew at ease, then let them have it."

"Since we are tapping into the stores…" Bitar said.

"That's enough, Adira," the captain said. "Masters Dufor and Alsahar, after the meal, please go to the hold and fetch a barrel of wine and bring it up to…"

"Orad and Suud," Reno finished.

"The best we have," the captain said.

"Yessir," I said. "I should be able to figure that out." I took my seat at the end of the long table and ladled out a bowl of warm porridge.

"This may be last warm meal for a while," Captain Azpa said. "Seas are getting worse. Majid will dampen the flames in the galley until after the storm."

In mid-Panis this far north the evenings were getting cool. The thought of being wet and cold with nothing but dried sausage and hardtack didn't sound appealing.

After the meal, Cort and I climbed below deck and found a barrel of Laetian red as large around as I was. The barrel was wedged into a dark corner of the hold near where the crew slept. We had to move five barrels of cheaper Drakkan wine out of the way get at it.

"What are they going to do with this, anyway?" I asked.

"Have you never seen a Sailor's Prayer before?" Cort said.

"Heard of it, but never seen one in person," I said. It was only half true, I had never heard of it either.

"Once we get this thing topside, go up to the quarterdeck. You'll want to watch it from there," he said.

The two of us wrestled the barrel to the ladder, placed it the netting, and used a line run through a block in the rigging to hoist the net and barrel up to the main deck.

We rolled the cask across the deck to where Orad Bah and Suud Amari were waiting. Fawz Khouri and Tamal Shandy were standing nearby, each holding a large fish, fresh from the sea and still fighting.

We set the barrel upright on the deck, and I looked up at Suud. He gave me a solemn nod and spoke. "Go stand with the others on the quarterdeck, Master Alsahar. This is not something for the officers."

I climbed the ladder with Cort and joined Lieutenant Bitar and Captain Azpa near the tiller. Both already wore their oilskins, ready for the impending rain.

Suud Amari stood shirtless before the mast, looking out toward the forecastle. His dark brown skin glistened with sweat. His black hair tousled in the increasing wind. In his right hand was a dagger, the same one that pierced my ribcage not a span ago. He shouted over the wind and the waves, "Blessings upon you, Father, Lord of the Deep. We are but humble sailors, cast upon your waves."

Suud pulled the dagger across the palm of his left hand, and blood ran down his arm. He reached out to the fish in Tamal's arms and smeared his blood across the head of the creature and shouted out to the water, "We ask for your protection, Lord Aequor."

Tamal raised the fish, covered in blood, above his head, then leaned over the larboard rail and dropped the fish into the sea.

Suud balled his left hand into a fist, and the blood dripped onto the deck. He walked across the deck to where Fawz stood with the other fish and repeated his prayer, covering the fish in his blood. Fawz raised the fish over his head, then leaned over the starboard rail and dropped his fish into the water.

Suud returned to the mast where Orad waited with an axe. "Lord Aequor, we offer you this gift and humbly ask that you watch over us. Protect us, until the day you call us home."

The dark-skinned sailor took the axe from his shipmate and drove it through the top of the barrel of wine, splintering it. Orad kicked over the barrel, and the dark crimson liquid spilled across the deck and over the sides of the ship.

The crew stood in silence as if waiting for a response. Suud waited, almost in a trance-like state. The seas grew ever more violent and the *Delilah Fritzbink* swayed in the heavy seas. The wind howled as a gust hit the ship from the starboard side. Our mainsail snapped and pulled taught. A large wave broke across the bow of the ship, sending water across the main deck and down the hatch into the hold. As if that was the answer he was expecting, Suud turned to the other crewmen and nodded.

"Fasten the hatches and raise the sail," Captain Azpa shouted. "Make ready for the gale."

"What about us?" I asked. "What should we do?"

The captain looked down to where Cort and I stood, "This will be a fierce storm. I want the two of you in your cabin until it is over."

I nodded to the captain. Sailors in the Sextant told stories of waves ripping men from the deck of a ship in a storm, never to be seen again. The last thing I wanted was to be on deck in a storm and gladly accepted the assignment.

Cort did not share my enthusiasm. He wanted to prove his mettle as a sailor to the captain and crew, to have them see him as an equal. For him, being sent below deck was an insult.

Headed to the hatch, Reno grabbed me by the arm. "Whatever you do, do not try to tap the *yili* of the gale. I don't care how strong you think you are. It will rip you apart."

I nodded to the war mage. *Did he think I would try to control storm? Could I?* Getting ripped apart did not sound particularly enjoyable.

Cort and I climbed down the ladder, and Orad pulled the wooden hatch over the hole and covered it with an oiled leather cover to keep the water out.

In the dark of the interior, we could hear Tomas as he laughed and drunkenly sang old sea songs in his cabin.

"At least it's an opportunity to rest," I said as I climbed into my hammock. "I haven't had a full night's sleep since we left home."

"Yeah, a good opportunity to sleep," Cort said. There was a slight shake to his voice, but in the darkness I couldn't tell if it was from anger or fear.

As I swayed back and forth in the hammock, I heard the muffled whimpers of the small boy in his bunk. Tough as he had to work on the ship, it was hard for me to remember that he was still just a boy of ten summers, far from his family.

"We'll be fine," I said. "This ship is the most reliable in the Empire's fleet."

There was a sniffle in dark. "You think so?"

"I know it," I said. "She's over a hundred years old and seen worse weather than this, I'm sure of it."

My mind raced as I lie awake in my hammock and swayed back and forth as the wind tossed the ship. One turn became a second and a third. Over the screaming winds and the thunderous waves I could hear Captain Azpa bellow orders to the crew. The occasional sniffle came from the rack beside me.

"Does your mother still live in Maropret?" I asked to break the silence and perhaps take his mind off the tossing ship.

"Uh huh," he said, "in Flat Bottom with my father."

"Was he a sailor too?" I asked.

"Night man," he said. "Ma didn't want her son mucking shit for some wealthy merchant. So when I turned eight, she marched me to the Southern Empire and offered to sell me to the company. A captain by the name of Helma Keets told her the Empire don't buy children, no matter the rumors. She offered my ma ten silver heads against my wages to work as a midshipman on her ship."

"Your mother tried to sell you?" I couldn't imagine Zori would ever try to sell me off, but my family has never been in such a position. In all my time as a student at the university, a wandering storyteller in Drakkas Port, or barback at the Sextant, I have never wanted for anything.

I want to go home.

"Yeah, but she didn't," he said. "So I sailed with Captain Keets for about a year on the *Dragon's Mercy*, a sloop running between Drakkas Port and Fortis. Then, one day, she announced she was leaving the Empire, resigning her post as captain. I was transferred to the *Delilah Fritzbink* and have been with Captain Azpa ever since. I think I have about another year, and I'll be ready to be a navigator on one of the small runners between Drakkas Port and the Inner Islands. Or maybe midshipman on a galleon head off to Jia loaded down with spices and gold on the way back."

"Jia is a dangerous haul. No one has been there in over a hundred years from what I hear," I said. "Beyond the Narrows and across the deadly Caligin Ocean."

The ship pitched, bow first, and a large wave crashed across the deck above us. The crew shouted now, reminded each other to hold on for their lives as each new wave crashed.

Tomas sang louder in his cabin as the waves broke around us. I pounded out the beat and joined in:

> *Farewell to you, my sweet Drakkan Ladies.*
> *Farewell to you, until I see you again.*
> *I sail with the tides to fight for the Emp're.*
> *I'll fight, and I'll die with all of my men.*
>
> *Hu'rah, Hu'rah to you Drakkan Ladies.*
> *Hu'rah, Hu'rah to your warm golden shores.*
> *With glory and gold we return to you, ladies.*
> *Once again ladies we'll darken your doors.*

The number of times I've led the house in a round of that song, the ale flying as sailors swayed and sang.

The ship pitched hard, and Cort heaved, the heavy seas just too much for him. He rushed to the basin in the corner of the cabin and spewed. *Just like back home.*

"Shit! Hold fast!" Bitar shouted from the decks above. "Hold fast!"

The ship dipped and rolled to the starboard side. Cort heaved again.

"Man overboard! Starboard side!" a shout from above.

"Hold Fast!" Bitar shouted again as another massive wave crashed over the ship.

"Wave! Hard to Larboard!" Azpa yelled over the storm and waves.

"Brace! Brace! Brace!" the crew yelled.

I remember it sounded like an explosion on the main deck. A thick shard of wood pierced the overhead, not more than a hand from where I lay. I flew from my hammock into the bulkhead. My head thrummed with pain. The world spun.

✱ ✱ ✱

The sun was warm on my face. Below me was solid soil. My eyes were closed, but I could hear the chattering of birds in the air. Peering out from heavy lids, I saw only a few wispy clouds in the brilliant blue of the sky.

I took in a deep breath. The sweet scent of fresh cut tobacco drying. I love that smell. It reminds me of family. Of home. Of sitting in the study with my father and brother as they discussed the happenings of the city.

I looked to my side. I was in the grass, a stone's throw from Merrywood, the plantation where my brother lived, just outside the massive walls of the city. The tobacco fields had been in my family for generations, a thousand years at least, handed down from father to son. When Ignis refused to leave the University, my grandfather gave the lands to Dukhan, my brother, instead.

Duk inherited the Merrywood ten years before the Collapse. At seventy-five, he was the youngest Alsahar to be master of the plantation. He toiled in the fields, cared for each plant. It showed in the finest gnomish tobacco ever grown in the Auster Islands, perhaps the world.

The year he turned eighty an imperial missive arrived from Fortis to his surprise. The emperor planned to winter in the Black Keep, as usual, and requested Dukhan provide enough loose tobacco and rolled cigars for the winter court. He was to be the Imperial Tobacconist. A position short lived. Fortis fell, and the emperor vanished. All that happened years before I was born.

I sat up, grass stuck to my hair and back. The clouds grew darker, not clouds, smoke. Thick columns of black smoke rose from the drying house across the field. The sweet smell of tobacco mixed with the scent of rot as a hot wind blew across the fields. Through the black smoke peered the terrible scaled face of a red dragon in armor.

From the fields marched men in the red tunics of the army, sword in one hand, shield in the other.

The massive serpent reared back its head and released a jet of fire at my family home. The flames licked at the yellow lapboard which quickly charred and caught, sending the fire deeper into the home. Soon fire engulfed the entire home. Somewhere beyond the house I heard screams. I tried to stand. Tried to run toward the screams. I couldn't move. I looked to the fields. The soldiers were closer now, led by a hulking man with golden plumage that erupted from the top of his gleaming helmet. It was Dem.

Dem looked down at me and cocked his head to the side as if he was considering what to do. Then he sneered, an intensity visible even beneath his helmet. His brilliant steel sword glinted in the warm sun as it pierced my chest.

CHAPTER TWENTY-ONE

"He still has breath. Go fetch water!" The smooth Laetian accent of the medic standing somewhere nearby pierced my mind. Beyond him I could hear water crash against the hull. Everything sat at odd angles in the darkness.

"Slow, slow, slow," Tomas said.

I tried to open my eyes, but my face throbbed with pain. I winced and tried to sit up. A white-hot pain shot from neck and across my chest.

"Try to relax," the doctor said.

"What—what's going on?"

"The ship was damaged in the storm," Tomas said. "You were injured. I need you to lay back and try to relax."

My breathing was quick, panicked. "Tomas, I can't see."

"I will clean you up and see how bad your injuries are," he said.

Behind him I could hear someone enter the cabin, heavy footfalls on the planks of the deck, a sloshing of water. A cold, wet rag moved gently across my face, mixed with a stinging pain on the right side.

"You are lucky, my friend! You will get to keep your eye," he said as he placed his broad hand across my face and muttered an incantation.

Warm, white energy filled my vision as the biomancer tried to heal my wounds. I blinked as he pulled his hands away. Tomas's eyelid and cheekbone had swollen over his left eye. Behind him Lurco Manos, the ship's master carpenter, held a bucket of water, his face contorted with worry.

Tomas pulled away a rag, red with blood, and reached into the bucket to soak it again. "I need to see how bad the cut on your chest is."

I glanced down. My white linen shirt was a dark crimson and stuck to my chest. In one quick motion, Tomas ripped the shirt open and I could see the blood seeping from a gash across my chest. My breath quickened again at the sight of so much blood.

"I need to make sure there is no debris in the wound before we try to seal it," he said. "This will hurt."

I leaned back, prepared for the pain. I felt hands of the rotund doctor pressing around the wound. Each jab an excruciating bolt through my body.

"As I thought — there are splinters in here," Tomas said. "Brace yourself."

I rolled my head back to brace for the pain. As I looked into the cabin, I saw crimson covered the space. A pool of dark, red blood pooled near the middle of the cabin. I followed the stream back toward its source. My eyes met the blue eyes of the young midshipman, a cold, unmoving stare.

My chest felt like Tomas stood on it. Every breath was an ordeal. I tried to sit up just as the fat fingers of Tomas slid into the gaping wound on my chest and removed a splinter as long as my hand. I screamed until my throat burned. Searing white pain flooded my vision as he ripped a piece of the ship from my chest. I closed my eyes against the pain, but I still saw Cort, lifeless on the deck. Blood ran from his mouth into a pool in the middle of the cabin floor.

Tomas muttered an incantation and pressed his palm into my chest. The warm energy of his magic sealed my wounds but left the pain.

* * *

Lurco and Tomas helped me to my feet. The deck listed hard to the larboard which added to the difficulty my broken body had with balance.

"Had a breach of the hull, just below the waterline. We've taken on some water," Lurco explained as I struggled to stand.

"That can't be good," I said, one hand on each of my rescuers. I wanted to turn around, turn toward Cort. I could feel the eyes stare at me as I stood.

"The hole's patched, but we'll need help to bail the bilge," the master carpenter said. "Cap'n sent me below to get you. That's when I found you two like this."

I noticed the fresh scars on Lurco's right arm, bright against his olive skin. He held the arm in a cautious pose to protect the fresh wounds.

"What about—" I couldn't bring myself to even say it.

"I will see to Master Dufor," Tomas said, "see that he is cleaned and prepared for proper burial."

Lurco bowed his head and gave a somber nod. "He was a good sailor. We'll take care of him."

With careful handholds on the bulkhead I could balance myself and make my way down the corridor to the ladder, bloody shirt torn from my chest. Every step of the ladder brought a new pain. My chest still felt every bit of the gouge closed only moments earlier. My hands left bloody palm prints on the walls and the ladder—my own blood or that of young Cort I didn't know.

My eyes peered above the hatch. I surveyed the damage. The rigging laid strewn around the deck and over the splintered rails into the water. The storm ripped half the forecastle from the bow and was missing.

Where the mast of the *Delilah Fritzbink* once stood there was now only a nest of splinters, broken off a fathom above the deck. On the quarterdeck, Jabnit muscled the sharp, jagged spear that had once been the tiller. It was the first time in nearly two span I had seen anyone other the Lieutenant Bitar at the helm.

Jabnit and I were the only two crew members on the deck. I had half expected most of the crew to be running about when I came topside. Instead I found it grave still.

The wind was gentle in the gray skies. The water lapped the bruised sides of the ship.

I raised my hand to wave to the fighter-turned-helmsman, but as my arm reached shoulder height, I could feel muscles in my chest tear against themselves. I let out a pitiful shout, doubled over and spat a glob of crimson blood onto the deck.

"You live. Good," Jabnit said in his broken imperial. "Captain is in his chamber."

"Where is everyone?" I asked, though somewhere deep inside I knew the answer.

Jabnit just shook his head, his lips pulled tight against his tusks. "Captain is expecting you."

I nodded and crossed the deck, slow and deliberate in my movements, to the officers' mess and the captain's chambers.

As I entered the officers' mess, I could hear hushed conversation in the next room. I stared at the empty chair at the end table. I thought of the shaggy haired boy with bright eyes and the enthusiasm for the sea. Thought of his broken body, crumpled now beneath my feet. What would they say to his mother? What would his mother, who once tried to sell him for a handful of coin, say when she learned he would never return to her?

I pushed open the door to the aft chamber.

Claudio Azpa, a patch over his left eye, stood and offered a warm smile as he saw me enter, "Thank the gods you are alive."

"I wish I could say the same for Cort," I said. Tears welled up in my eyes.

"He was a good man," Reno said.

"A good sailor," Claudio corrected.

"A lot of good that gets you," I snapped.

"He knew the risks, same as all of us," Claudio said. "And he was not the only one we lost. Five men were swept overboard in the storm."

I looked around the small table the Captain used as a desk. Reno held his arm with care, the same way the master carpenter had below. Majid, the ship's cook, had a blackened eye and bandages covered his right arm.

Tredway, one of the two lookouts on the forecastle, still had blood in his hair and purplish-red rope burns on either arms. I saw no sign of his counterpart, Bek Bly, who I knew from the Sextant.

Kane Cloud, the burly Aeromonian sailmaker had his head wrapped in thick bandages. Fawz Khouri, the fisherman and deckhand I had helped when I first started my rounds with Tomas, sat with his bandaged leg propped on a chest he shared with Elazaro Wion, the carpenter whose foot I crushed in combat just days before.

Not a single member of the *Fritzbink* crew, nor even the ship herself, had escaped damage.

"Lieutenant Bitar?" I asked.

"Alive. She is below with the doctor," Captain Azpa said. "She had a piece of the tiller sticking out of her chest when Reno pulled her over the rail. Even with the timber in her, she held fast."

✳ ✳ ✳

The ship sat low in the water. Waves broke on the deck, and the breach in the hull had filled the lowest portions of the ship. Correcting the heavy list of the ship was the priority for the survivors. The sea was still choppy after the gale and large waves broke over the larboard side. A tall enough wave could pull the *Delilah Fritzbink* under.

As the only remaining crew member small enough to crawl into the ballast chamber and bilge, the Captain relegated the task to me.

"It is a cranking device with pipe fittings on either side," Claudio explained as we moved to the ladder. "The pump should be fastened to the bulkhead on the larboard side of the ballast chamber."

I stepped off the bottom rung and into water. *The water level has risen since I was topside.* I sloshed through the putrid smelling water toward the bow, tried to locate the ladder to the ballast chamber. Crates and barrels once arranged with care now floated free. Most of the cargo from the starboard side slid into the central walkway and forced the ship even further on her side.

The ladder down was along the starboard side, a stack of crates collapsed over the opening. I maneuvered between the crates and the bulkhead and down the ladder. As the water reached my chest, I took a deep breath of the foul-smelling air.

I dipped below the water. Darkness. A wet, silent grave. The overhead was low, a cubit and a half at the tallest spot. Hand over hand I pushed along the beam, a full fathom to the larboard bulkhead. I swiped my hand and hoped to find the pump. Nothing. Pushed further back. Waved again. Nothing but the old tarred timbers. My lungs burned. I had to find the pump. Pushed back and swept again. A sharp pain in my hand. Splintered wood. The hull was breached, hidden below the water. I kicked off the bulkhead toward the faint light of the ladder.

I exploded out of the water, gasping for breath. My head struck the crates fallen over the ladder.

"Lurco!" I shouted as loud as my burning lungs would allow. The master carpenter heard my shouting and pushed his way to where I floated.

"How did you get down there?" He asked as he heaved massive wooden crates away from the hatch.

"Breach," I said, spitting water. "We've got a hull breach, larboard side, about two fathoms back from the ladder."

The brown eyes of the carpenter narrowed. "I knew there had to be another." He darted away from the hatch and returned a moment later with a few pieces of wood and a red mage lamp sealed in a glass jar.

He handed the lamp to me, "You hold this while I patch. Ready?"

I nodded, took a deep breath, and dove below the water. Lurco followed. His massive body cramped and constrained in the narrow space. With the aid of the light, I looked around for the pump. Nothing. There was a gap in the timbers of the bulkhead, opened out to the great expanse of darkness.

Lurco took his two pieces of lumber fastened in the middle with a bolt. He shifted the piece so he could slide one to the outside the ship and the other to the interior.

As Lurco worked to seat the patch to cover the breach, I spotted a thin line which ran from the bulkhead out the breach. I tapped Lurco to get his attention, then pulled on the line. It was heavy, something attached to the end outside the ship. I pulled harder, and the pump glinted in the red light of the mage lamp. Hand over hand I pulled in the pump and set it aside. Lurco motioned his approval and seated the patch. My lungs burned with pain as we spun a wooden crossbar attached to the bolt and tightened the wooden patch into place. I grabbed the pump, removed the line, and kicked off the bulkhead back toward the hatch.

I broke the surface of the water with a gasp and threw the pump on the deck, then clamored to get clear of the ladder. A second later Lurco emerged from the water, coughing up water onto the deck.

"This day was almost much worse," he said in his thick Maropretian accent. "Glad you found that pump."

"I need to get this to the Captain," I climbed to my feet and hefted the brass pump.

"Tell them to send anyone who can walk down here," Lurco said. "We need to balance the cargo."

I pushed through the cluttered lower deck until I reached the sunlight of the ladder to the main deck. Brass pipes from the deck to the bottom of the hold were already in place. I handed the pump to Reno and Majid. Elazaro and Jabnit headed below to help balance the cargo. With the pump connected to the pipes, Reno cranked the device and water rushed over the side.

I climbed on the quarterdeck. Captain Azpa had taken over the helm. I sat on the ladder. Soaked to the skin and bare-chested, I stared out to the hazy gray horizon and began to shiver. My chest and my face throbbed with pain. I reached up to touch the right side of my face and found a ridge of fresh scar tissue from my jaw to the hairline.

"I should have been in the rack," I said. "Cort should have been in the hammock. He offered."

"Lady Nex will come for you, too, one day, just like she comes for each of us," the Captain said, his voice just perceptible over the crashing waves and the water pump. "Today was not your day. We lost six good sailors. I fear we will lose more before we return home. All that matters is that you do everything you can between now and the day she comes for you."

CHAPTER TWENTY-TWO

The sun was low in the sky by the time the ship leveled. The fading light cast the sea with the same reds and oranges of the horrific morning. The skies had cleared and winds had softened to a dull breeze. Had we any sails, they would have gently fluttered, almost still.

Tomas brought a dry change of clothes up from my cabin, and Captain Azpa had offered his cabin to change. I accepted the folded bundle and brought them into the warm chambers at the aft of the ship.

Compared to its earlier comfort, the Captain's cabin looked as though someone had ransacked it, armoire knocked over, ledgers and maps strewn about the room. I righted a chair and placed the dry clothes in a careful pile. I stood in silence, and stared at the pile of borrowed clothes. The bloodied and torn rags that clung to my body were his too.

Cort had every right to object to my intrusion. I had stolen from him the only privacy he had on the ship, his sanctuary. And he gave it up willingly. With enthusiasm he shared his clothes, his food, his fears. At ten years old Cort was a finer sailor—a better person—than I could hope to become. *And yet he rests down there while I must continue.*

Perhaps Claudio was right. "You must do everything you can until your day comes."

But where is the justice? What justice is there in the death of a child? I took a deep breath. My chest burned with pain as it heaved.

I strode to the Captain's basin and rinsed the blood off my face, hands, and body. The dark brown of my skin, split in so many places with fresh scars, gave way to deep purples of bruises.

My black hair was a tangled and blood-caked mess. I rinsed my hair in the bowl, turning the water crimson. I dried myself with a towel and combed my hair back. I touched the deep scar on my face—a mark of shame. *He died, and I lived.*

I pulled off my wet, bloody clothes and dropped them into a pile on the floor, exchanged them for the warmth of the cotton shirt, the woolen tunic, and a pair of breeches that just barely fit.

* * *

When I returned to the main deck, the remainder of the crew gathered. On a plank along the larboard side lay the body of Cort, cleaned and dressed in his finest uniform.

Tomas motioned for me to join him. I hesitated, then quietly moved to stand next to the doctor.

Claudio stepped up to the body and leaned down. With a quick motion, he removed the midshipman insignia both Cort and I wore. In its place was a different insignia, the mark of Merchant Ensign.

"In the event of a death in service to the Company," Tomas whispered, "a promotion is automatically granted. Master Zori's orders."

I looked up. My brow furrowed.

"To award higher death benefits to your family," he said.

While the Captain affixed the new rank to the boy's small uniform, Reno adjusted something at the feet. Claudio looked to Reno, who nodded and stood to attention.

"Ensign Cort Dufor of Maropret died in service the Southern Empire Trading Company," Captain Azpa said. "Though we commit his body to the deep, we ask Lady Nex to guide his spirit to a peaceful slumber."

As the Captain and the Sergeant each held a side of the plank near the boy's head, I glimpsed what Reno had placed at his foot. The men lifted the plank at an angle, and a large stone tied to the foot slid over the rail and into the water. The rope snapped taut, the body slid from the plank, and crashed into the sea. The stone pulled the boy below the waves.

My eyes burned as tears ran down my face, but I dared not move.

After a moment of silence Tredway Persson, the lookout, came forward, holding a folded uniform.

"Boatswain's Mate Bek Bly, I commit your body to the deep. May Lady Nex guide your soul," Captain Azpa said, and Tredway dropped the uniform into the sea.

Jabnit took to the rails next.

"Boatswain First Rate Graham Beut, I commit your body to the deep. May Lady Nex guide your soul." The Captain's eye reddened as one after another, a crewman took to the rails.

Cooper Orad Bah.

Carpenter First Rate Suud Amari.

Ropemaker First Rate Tamal Shandy.

"Blessings upon you, Father, Lord of the Deep. We are but humble sailors, cast upon your waves," Captain Azpa said, his voice cracking as he prayed. "Lord Aequor, god of the seas, we offer you these gifts and humbly ask that you watch over us. Protect us, until the day you call the rest of us home."

CHAPTER TWENTY-THREE

T he funeral concluded as the last light of the day slipped below the horizon. The *Fritzbink* drifted without direction on the sea. Tomas returned below deck to see to Lieutenant Bitar, while Captain Azpa, Reno, and I headed to the officers' mess. It had been turns since the last meal, but the thought of food only made the bile rise in my stomach.

I tried to avoid looking to the end of the table as I sat in Bitar's chair.

Captain Azpa flipped one of several timing devices mounted to the wall and gave it a good thump before he entered his cabin and returned with a roll of parchment.

"I will speak straight with you. We are dead in the water and do not know where we are." The Captain rolled a navigational chart of the Azurean Sea over the rough-hewn table.

"This is where we were when the storm struck," he pointed to a course plotted with care, drawn from Drakkas Port to a point one hundred and fifty leagues from Whyte Harbor.

Reno continued the calculations, "The storm came out of the southwest. From the time Jabnit spotted it on the horizon to the time it was on top of us was two turns. That's ten to fifteen knots, not enough to snap the mast."

"No," Claudio said, "But the wind inside the storm can be much faster than the gale itself. The highest ever reported to the Harbor Master in Drakkas Port was a hundred knots."

"We were within the storm for five turns," Reno said. "We could be anywhere in this area." He placed his thick hands in a wedge-shape on the map spread out from our last known position.

Deep furrows formed on Claudio's forehead as he frowned.

"That's half the damn Azurean!" I shouted.

"Only a quarter," Claudio said as he studied Reno's hands on the map. "But we are within these latitudes?"

"Most certainly," Reno said.

The Captain turned and walked back to his cabin and returned with a thick book and a leather satchel.

He thumbed through the pages until he found the one he needed.

"It is the twenty-fourth day of Panis," He ran his finger over the page and looked to the timer on the wall and back to his book. "A half turn past sunset means the constellation Pallum should be between three and four marks above the eastern horizon. Shall we?"

The Captain set the book on the table and marched through the hatch to the main deck.

"I should have paid better attention to my helmsmanship lessons," I said as I rushed onto the main deck. "I have no idea what is happening."

"He's trying to determine our position based on the stars," Reno said.

The captain stood on the quarterdeck and looked out at the eastern horizon. Jabnit nodded to the captain from the splintered tiller.

Claudio reached into his leather satchel and retrieved a large brass sextant and held it up, first to his bandaged left eye out of habit then shifted it to his right eye and made a few adjustments to the device as Reno and I stood and watched.

He returned the sextant to his bag and pulled out a brass astrolabe and changed out the plates. He held the round device up to his eye, then examined the device. His brow furrowed and his mouth drew into a tight line.

He climbed down from the quarterdeck and returned to the officers' mess, Reno and I close behind. The Captain turned the map toward him at the table and studied it.

"Well, Reno, your estimation is superb," he said after several breathless moments. He walked over to the rack of timing devices, and as the last grains of sands left the upper glass, he flipped it back over.

He returned to the map and pointed at a spot east of Whyte Harbor. "Here is where we are."

"Ten Hells, Captain!" Reno shouted.

The spot under Captain Azpa's finger was two hundred leagues east of Whyte Harbor.

"So we make due west?" I asked.

"If we had a sail, perhaps," the Captain said. "But we are in the middle of the Azurean Current."

I shook my head.

"Ever wonder why shipments to Maropret go through Whyte Harbor?" Reno asked.

"Sure. Zori said it's faster than going east along Greater Auster," I said.

"That is because the Azurean Current is a powerful sea current that runs from Whyte Harbor to Maropret in the East and back along Greater Auster toward Drakkas Port. Whyte Harbor is the only island in the current, which helps with the speed. A ship leaving Whyte Harbor can reach Lesser Auster in four spans," Reno said.

"So now we're four spans from port instead of four days?" I understood the worry on their faces.

"Again," Captain Azpa said. "If we had a mast and a sail. Adrift on the current, it will take closer to two, maybe three months."

My stomach sunk, and my head spun. Two months adrift on the open sea.

"When we do not arrive in four days, the company will know there was a problem," Reno said. "The Harbor Master will look for us then."

"They will look for us south of Whyte Harbor," Claudio said. "They will find debris and assume we were lost in the storm."

"Seraplaun!" I swore.

"There's little we can do tonight," Captain Azpa said. "Everyone should try to rest. We will start to ration our food now."

"Water will be a problem, Captain," Reno said. "Most was tainted or spilled in the squall."

The furrow that seemed a permanent fixture on the captain's brow deepened. "We must hope for rain, or we drift past an uncharted island."

"Are there many uncharted islands on a major shipping lane?" I asked.

"A few, rocky outcroppings a few hundred leagues off the Nivalean coast," Reno said. "When I was younger, the ship they assigned me to use to make runs to Maropret. I remember the rocky shores covered in sea lions."

"So, what then?" I asked, "Hunt sea lions and hope for a passing ship?"

"We hope for an island with trees and sheep," Reno said. His laughter roared in the cabin as he slapped me on the back. "And beautiful native girls! Good night, gentlemen." With that hulking man headed toward the hatch.

"Captain," I said, my voice shook as I spoke. "I—I can't go back into that cabin. The blood—"

Claudio nodded and raised his hand before I could continue. "I understand your reservation all too well. We used the cabin space for cargo to help balance the ship. Majid and Fawz brought your hammock to my cabin. You are welcome to stay with me."

"In your cabin?"

"It is your ship, after all," he said.

I let out a deep breath, feeling the burden Claudio had carried. I forced a pained smile on my face, hoping to reassure him, "I can think of no better hands for her to be in, Captain. Thank you."

CHAPTER TWENTY-FOUR

The morning after the storm that killed half our crew, the sky was blue, and the seas were still. If Aequor existed, he seemed content with the tremendous sacrifice we gave him.

Along with my hammock, Majid and Fawz brought the remainder of Cort's clothes to the Captain's cabin. I spent half a turn examining the clothes, each stitch that mended a hole, each stain. It was all that was left of a life stripped away. I almost refused the clothing until I realized the shirt I was wearing was his. I spent a mark rinsing the salt water and blood from my hair and beard in the washbasin in the cabin and studying the endless number of new scars that now crossed my face, back, and chest. They reminded me of the faded scars on the arms of Old Herus back at the Rusted Sextant.

185

"Reminders of old friends," he used to say.

I ran a finger along the raised scar that ran across my right eye and down my cheek. *Old friends.*

My stomach twisted with hunger and ripped me from my thoughts. It had been a full day since the last meal. I rushed to put on a fresh linen shirt and a heavy, blue, woolen tunic.

As I stepped through the door of the captain's cabin into the officers' mess, Reno was giving the details of the damage.

"… rope and canvas to rig a new sail, but without a mast we will not get very far. Pumping the hold took most of the night, but the hull is watertight again, though damaged."

The tattooed man paused for a moment. Lack of sleep darkened his eyes. He drew a deep breath and then continued, "Half our food stores are waterlogged or pulled overboard in the storm. Majid says we have twelve days of stores, a month if we go to half rations. Fresh water looks to run out well before that. We have perhaps a span remaining."

"We have plenty of water," I said. "Isn't there a way to pull salt out of seawater, to make it drinkable? You know, through arcane means?"

"None that I know," Claudio shrugged.

I sighed. "Well, what about the cargo?" I asked as a sat in my chair at the end of the table. Bitar was absent. "Is there anything we can eat out of the cargo? Our lives are more important than the cargo at this point."

Reno's eyes shot to the Captain who responded, "Nothing we can eat—farm tools headed for the outer islands. A good thought though. Doctor, how is the crew?"

Tomas wiped the crumbs from his bruised face and cleared his throat. "Of the remaining crew, not a one of us escaped uninjured. Some are more superficial than others. We have missing eyes, lacerations, and broken bones. I am afraid Adira is in the worst shape, broken ribs, a broken arm, multiple deep lacerations. With help, I could have most of the crew back to work in a few days."

The doctor's eyes moved from me to the captain.

Claudio nodded as he rubbed his brow. "I agree. Master Alsahar, I would put your talents to use with Doctor Flores. Sergeant Leon, Lurco and Elazaro could use an extra set of hands on repairs."

"Aye, Captain," the hulking brute said.

I nodded. I was still in pain, and the opportunity to remain busy would help clear my mind.

"Our first patient of the day will be the Captain," Tomas said from across the table.

"Nevermind my eye," Claudio said. He turned his head away from the doctor. "See to the others first."

"As you wish," the doctor said with a nod, "but the sooner we begin the process, the sooner you will be back to good health."

"You have relieved the pain, that is enough for now," the Captain said.

* * *

After the meager meal of hardtack and dried meat, Tomas and I headed below deck.

"Can you regrow his eye?" I asked as we descended the ladder below decks. The air stunk of fresh tar and sea water.

"Repair is possible, yes," the doctor said. "But the longer we take to begin, the more difficult it will be."

As my eyes adjusted to the dark interior, I could see the crew arranged much of the cargo in the hold to leave an open area where they moved their hammocks.

Forward of the new sleeping area, the crew gathered in the galley.

"How much work's he expect us to do on half rations?" Kane Cloud asked to his shipmates. The large sailmaker sat at a table, his head still wrapped in thick bandages.

"There is little work to be done," said Elazaro, the one-eyed carpenter. "And if we are on half rations, it means the Captain thinks we are far off course."

Tomas cleared his throat, and the group gathered around the table turned to look at him. "I will check on the Lieutenant. Master Alsahar will tend to some of your wounds."

The single eye of the carpenter widened as he remembered my last attempt to heal his foot. He opened his mouth to object, but Tomas turned and walked off before he could utter a word.

"Well," I said as I surveyed my patients. "Who's first?"

Elazaro shook his head and pushed away from the table. He made his way deeper into the galley to help Majid organize the stores.

"Kane, how about you?" I said as I climbed atop a crate to get eye level with the sailmaker.

He helped remove the bandages from around his head, red and wet closer to his skull. I inspected the wound. He had a deep, bloody gash within his hair.

"Doc said he was out of magic yesterday," Kane said as I continued my examination. "Best he could do was wrap me up."

I closed my eyes and searched for the sailmaker's *yili.* A faint yellow spark glinted in the darkness. I drew a deep breath and connected to his energy. I set my *sebi* on the gash, focused on drawing the energy of the small spark to the wound. As the energy pulled to the top of his head, I uttered the incantation I had learned in the *Medela.*

The large man gave a sharp inhale as his wound closed. Sensing the procedure complete, I opened my eyes to see the fresh scar on the top of his head.

"There you are," I said. "It'll hurt for a few days, but you didn't break bones—just a deep cut."

Kane ran a finger along the scar, his fingers crimson from the blood in his hair. He looked up at me and smiled. "That might have been better than the Doc!" He stood up—his head almost reaching timbers in the overhead—gathered up his bloody bandages, and headed to a pile of canvas sails further forward.

"So, who's next?" I asked as the remaining crew studied me. "Tredway?"

The fair-haired lookout was almost to the ladder up to the main deck when he stopped short. "These?" he asked motioning to the rope burns on his arms. "Not worth your time, sir. I've had worse climbing the rigging." Before I could respond he was up the ladder.

"Fawz? How's your leg?" I turned my attention to the Drakkan steward. The doctor had bandaged his left leg, and he moved with a deliberate limp.

I motioned for him to take a seat, and climbed off the crate. Once seated, I helped unwrap the injuries. As the bandages came off, I could smell the sour scent of infection in the wound. My brow furrowed and the steward could sense my concern.

"What is it?" he asked.

"I need my book."

"It's just a wound, just like Kane," he said. "Can't you do the same thing?"

I grabbed the bandages and pressed them back on to the wound. "Hold this here and don't move."

"What's wrong? It's just a simple wound, right?"

I left the galley and headed toward the doctor's chamber where I had left the copy of *Medela*. As I passed Lieutenant Bitar's cabin there was a loud pop, followed by a muffled scream as Tomas set a bone. Not wanting to interrupt, I continued down the corridor. I froze motionless at the hatch to my cabin. I stared at the closed door. The thought of the cabin filled my mind. The lifeless blue eyes of Cort staring at me. I could feel the bile rise in my throat.

I used the burning sensation as a distraction and pushed into the doctor's cabin and found the medical text. Taking a deep breath, I ran back to the crew's mess to continue treatment.

Fawz was still panicked when I returned and placed the book on the table beside him. I thumbed through pages until I found the section on infections and skimmed it. The steward attempted to look over my shoulder at the text.

"What does it say?" he asked.

"How to heal your leg," I said with a smile. "Ready?"

He furrowed his brow, his eyes wide.

"No."

I closed my eyes and took a deep breath. His *yili* was not the bright, pulsing energy I had seen just a span before. Like Kane, Fawz's *yili* was now dim. This wound was killing him. If he had waited another day, it may cost him his leg or his life. I set my *sebi* on the gouge in his leg and whispered the incantation to close the wound. The faint *yili* drew close to wound but was not strong enough reach.

With a sharp breath I let my consciousness sink into an almost trance-like state. The ship bobbed back and forth on the gentle seas. The waves broke against the battered hull.

This is a bad idea. It could kill him. If I didn't do it, he could be dead by morning.

I pulled the *yili* from the crashing waves inside me, then channeled that energy into Fawz.

Somewhere in the distance I could hear people talking. Deep in my meditative state it only sounded like hushed muttering. I could see his dim *yili* grow brighter as the energy flowed into him. I tied my *sebi* to his wound and forced the warm energy into closing his wound. With the incantation the wound closed, and I focused on the infection. It looked like thick, dark spots on the threads of the Fabric. The infection was spreading through his body. I uttered the incantation to revert infection. The bright *yili* reached out in many directions, touched each of the dark spots and banished them.

A heavy hand clasped my shoulder as I released the trance.

"Master Alsahar, a word in my chamber please?" the doctor said behind me.

As I opened my eyes, the crew all stared at me. Fawz sat still with tears running down his cheeks.

"Now," the doctor said.

I stood and followed the rotund doctor back toward his cabin, my attention on the sweat stain on the back of his tunic to keep the thoughts of Cort's body from my mind. He slammed the door shut as I stepped into the room.

"What the fuck did you think you were doing?"

I raised an eyebrow at the objection. "Saving his life. His wounds were infected, and he was slipping away. Another day, and he would have been gone."

"You never attempt to push *yili* into a patient. Ever. You could kill him."

"The infection would have killed him."

"You could have killed both of you. If he does not have the *yili*, you treat him the best you can with mundane methods. It is not for us to decide who lives and who dies."

My eyes widened in realization.

"You know they will die."

"That is ridiculous."

"You told them it was you, that you didn't have the magic to cure them. But this whole time you knew — Kane, Fawz, and how many others? That they would die, and you did nothing to stop it, that's why you could revive me even after you told them you were depleted. But why would you ask for my help if you knew?"

Tomas's mouth drew into a tense line, and he studied me before responding. "It is a lesson every biomancer must learn. You are powerful, but you are no match for death."

He walked behind his bed to the console against the far wall and poured himself a glass of whiskey. "You, boy, are perhaps the most powerful caster I have ever heard of, able to cast in the schools of Illusion, Biomancy, Elementalism, and Arkanus knows what else, as though you were breathing."

He sat down in his chair and sipped his whiskey. "It was four years before I could harness my own *yili*. You mastered it in an afternoon. Headmaster Yani'ral of the Laetian Imperial College could cast magic from four schools after eight hundred years of study. And the spoiled boy who falls onto my ship can use three after, what, two spans?" He let out a deep, maniacal laugh.

"You are indeed powerful, Ferrin," he said, "but you need to learn that you are no god. You need to learn that death does not care how strong you think you are."

I stared in silence at the corpulent, red-faced doctor sipping his whiskey. The muscles in my jaw tensed as I ground my teeth. Without saying a word I left the cabin and slammed the hatch closed behind me.

I clenched my fists so tight as I climbed the ladder out of the hold my hands dripped blood onto the deck where my fingernails had broken the skin. I felt lightheaded as I reached the door to the officers' mess.

Reno spotted me from the demolished forecastle, dropped the lumber, and rushed toward me.

"Let it out, boy, or it will kill you!" he shouted.

He struck my back with his massive palm. The jolt sent my head back, and I looked up to the sky. As the last air in my lungs passed my lips, I thought an arcane word, and the sky erupted in flames that stretched to the horizon.

CHAPTER TWENTY-FIVE

I stood on the broken main deck of the *Fritzbink* and looked out over the waves. Small rocky islands, half the size of the ship appeared on the horizon as the current pulled us along.

"You are supposed to be helping Doctor Flores," Reno approached the damaged rail.

"I'm holding clinic hours on the deck. The fresh air is good for the—something."

"It smells foul down there, I will give you that," he said. "This have to do with that explosion a few days ago?"

It had been almost a span since I even looked in the hatch's direction to the lower decks. "How can he—If I knew you were sick, would you want to know?"

"Can you heal this sick?"

"Maybe — not how Flores works, but —"

"If nothing can be done about it, why worry?" He handed me a sword belt with a dagger. "You should worry about your parries."

On the quarterdeck above us, Jabnit held the broken tiller. His dark, sunken eyes searched the horizon for any sign of aid — land or another vessel.

I fastened the leather belt around my waist. Each day the belt seemed to fit looser than the last. On the larger men the days of partial meals and meager fresh water had taken their toll — hollow faces and lean bodies. My ribs showed when I removed my shirt at night.

I moved to the center of the main deck for a sparring session with the master-at-arms. The dagger felt like an anchor in my hands. I moved through the first set of War Dance forms but had to rest each time I raised the blade above my head.

"That's about all I can handle right now." My muscles burned by the time we finished the third set. My movement through the forms was sluggish.

"Can you capture enough *yili* to raise the wind?" Reno asked when he had seen enough.

A pang in my stomach hit harder than any blow from Jabnit.

"The only think I can thing about is food," I said.

"Sebi. Yili. Agoti," the war mage said.

I closed my eyes and focused on the waves.

Nothing.

I could go for a bowl of goat stew. I sat down on the deck next to Reno.

"That is enough for today," he said.

Neither of us moved.

"How long until supper?"

"It is just now midday."

"Fuck."

CHAPTER TWENTY-SIX

Eleven days after the storm, with an impotent healer at her side, Adira Bitar succumbed to her wounds.

Days later Kane Cloud would tell me she had begged for death, pleaded with anyone who could hear her meek cries for mercy. Not wanting to upset the work of the gods, the good doctor offered her only a glass of whiskey from his private stash and waited until the infection took her.

When they brought her body onto the deck for her funeral, her face still wore the mask of agony she must have experienced in her final days. Her body carried the putrid scent of infection and necrosis.

The captain stood on the deck in his dress uniform. Even with the eyepatch he could not hide his worried, dark eyes and gaunt face. He replaced the insignia on Adira's collar with the rank of commander before asking once again for mercy and safe passage from the sea god that had no interest in our return home.

Tomas Flores did not attend Bitar's funeral, perhaps out of guilt for his inaction, perhaps out of the justified fear I would provide a more suitable sacrifice to Aequor. He did not come to the officers' mess for the evening meal, if you could consider half a hardtack and a swallow of fresh water a meal. And so he was not present when Claudio called a meeting of the ship's officers during the meal.

"Drakkan maritime law is clear on matters of the chain of command," the captain's dry, graveled voice betrayed his smooth Laetian accent. "Every ship flying a Commonwealth flag must have a captain and first mate. And while we no longer have a mast, nor the flag atop, we are a Drakkan ship. Sergeant Reno Leon, would you do the *Delilah Fritzbink* the honor of being her first mate?"

I turned to the master-at-arms, my face beamed with the first joy I'd felt in several spans.

The massive man laughed as ran his tattooed hands over his blood red tunic to straighten it. He grumbled to the captain, "Not if it came with ten minutes alone with Erista and her sisters."

"Why in ten hells not?" The words escaped my mouth before I had even realized I was speaking.

The brute lowered his head and sighed, "I swore I would never take a command again. It is on you."

The captain nodded and turned to face me, "Midshipman Ferrin Alsahar, do you accept command of the *Delilah Fritzbink* as her first mate?"

This is the moment Zori had always wanted. The decades misspent on arcane studies, the moving from alehouse to seedy alehouse telling stolen tales of adventures. No manner of hiding at the bottom of a barrel can protect you from the life the Fates chose for you.

Reno nodded his head from across the table, eyes fixed on me.

I blew out the breath in my chest. "Yeah, I guess so," my hands thrown up in resignation.

The brute shot me a wide grin in approval.

"Then I do hereby promote you to the rank of Lieutenant of the Southern Empire Trading Company and name you first mate of the *Delilah Fritzbink*." The Captain extended his hand, and as I clasped it discovered he palmed an insignia, which he handed off in the handshake. "Congratulations, Lieutenant."

* * *

It was already dark when I stepped from the officers' mess on to the main deck. The sun had grown as lethargic as the half-starved crew in the northern latitudes. The night was crisp, and I could see my breath in the red mage light.

I climbed the ladder to the quarterdeck. "Go grab some food and rest, Jabnit." I said motioning to the orc at the tiller.

"Very well…" he paused and cocked an eyebrow, taking notice of the insignia change on my tunic. "Lieutenant? You rise quickly."

He nodded and maneuvered down the ladder and toward the hatch below deck with care. Gone was the nimble orc who danced with effortless ease in the rigging. A span and a half of cut rations led to aches and pains, frayed nerves, and short tempers. Jabnit, ever seeking efficiency and balance, hid the latter better than most.

I took hold of the splintered spar and attempted to get my bearings.

The warm light of the officers' mess illuminated the main deck as Reno stepped out into the cold night air. The deck dimmed again, and he climbed up to the quarterdeck. He leaned against the aft rail beside the tiller and looked out over the dark sea.

After a few marks of silence he asked, "Any idea where we are going?"

"Not a clue."

"Even know which direction we are pointed?"

"You know, it's more of a formality," I said with a laugh. "I have little say in the matter."

"I am glad we both understand that."

"You think that's why Jabnit likes it up here?"

"In times of extreme stress, the mind looks for anything normal to grasp hold of, a way to wrestle control back from the chaos," he said. "After one bloody battle I once saw a man strip down and take a bath in the town fountain."

"What?"

"He said he needed to get clean. To him, it was the only part of his world he could control at that moment. Trust me, the alternative is worse."

"Why did you turn down the first mate?"

In place of an answer, Reno looked over the water. It was the same look I sometimes got from Dem when we would talk about his campaigns.

"My mother always wanted me to join her in the family business," I said, hoping the change of subject would bring Reno back from wherever my abrupt question had sent him. "She hoped, one day maybe a hundred years from now, I'd take over Southern Empire when she decided it was time to try something new. Father hoped I would become an Archmage at the University like him. He was so disappointed when the mages assigned me to Illusion."

"And what did you want to do?" the soldier asked, turning his attention from the dark horizon.

"Drink and fuck," I said with a chortle.

Reno snorted at my honesty. "If I had the coin your family has, there would not be a dry keg or a straight-legged woman in the Commonwealth."

"Believe me, I gave it my best go," I said. "But I haven't seen a stray pin from my family in years. I wanted to prove I could make it on my own, that I could do whatever I wanted, without the family wealth. I slept in a piss-soaked bed above the Rusted Sextant or the room of whichever woman or man I'd, uh, befriended the night before."

Reno cocked an eyebrow at me.

"I wanted to be an adventurer," I continued, "like the heroes of the Age of Legend I read about. Go to distance lands, fight great evils, rescue the damsel in the tower."

"In my experience, the damsel can rescue her own damn self," Reno said.

"I wanted to be a soldier, like my best friend, Dem," I said. "Lead missions to bring food and supplies to starving farmers in the Outer Islands."

Reno bellowed a laugh, "Maropret? Is that what they told you back in Drakkas Port?"

"Sure, Dem told me all about how the army brought food and medicine to Maropret to help the starving farmers," I said.

"Listen, I do not know about your friend Dem, but that's not how I remember Maropret," Reno said.

"What do you mean?"

"The farmers on Maropret were starving. The island had been in a drought for two years before we ever arrived. Food and supplies were being shipped in by merchants, but the Vizier of Maropret decided to hoard the grain, meats, and medicines, dispersing them only to the noble families of the island. The month before we arrived, the riots began. Starving farmers, merchants, women, and children," he said.

"So you arrested the Vizier?" I asked.

"You do not send ten ships filled with seasoned warriors and a battle-dressed dragon to smack a

Vizier on the fingers and hand out bags of grain," he said.

"My column was the first on the beach when we arrived. The dragon had already begun passes over the island. It torched dozens of farms, homes, whatever it could find.

"I remember there were no birds, no gulls around the port. No dogs barking as we marched inland. No cats around the warehouses hunting mice. They ordered us to march to the Vizier's Palace, so that is what we did. Rioting is illegal in the Commonwealth, so is looting. We cut down bone-thin farmers like stalks of wheat in Panis. In one home…"

Reno paused abruptly. I realized the brute was tearing up.

"In one home we found the foot and lower leg of a child next to a hearth. A woman standing over a fire, turning a spit with a roast on it. Children, some as young as Cort, wore pots and pans as armor, wielding kitchen knives against trained soldiers. I had to give the order to my men. They never stood a chance.

"The ruthless General Aurellis replaced the gluttonous Vizier. We executed men as young ten summers. The general handed women as young as eight summers over to the soldiers. 'We must maintain the island's population,' they told us. We wintered in Maropret.

"The new year saw rain for the first time in three years. My term was up by the time I returned to

Drakkas Port. I resigned my post and drank my pay, hoping I could forget what I had seen, what I had done. But you cannot forget such things. By the time I sobered up, I was on an Empire ship in the middle of the Azurean."

The knot in my stomach tightened. I wanted to vomit, but my stomach wanted desperately to hold on to the few scraps of stale bread it had. "But all those stories from Dem," my voice shook as I spoke.

"We tell our loved ones what they need to hear sometimes," he said, "because we could never bear what they would think of us if they knew the truth."

Reno let out a breath that held the weight of years of unspoken truths. "I swore to myself I would never take a command again."

I stood in silence at what this truth could mean. *Did that mean that Dem —*

"Mast off the larboard bow," the cry ripped me from my thoughts.

"I have a bad feeling about this, Ferrin," Reno said. "Remember — *yili, sebi, agoti.*"

CHAPTER TWENTY-SEVEN

"What do you mean you have a bad feeling?" I scanned the dark horizon looking for the masts.

"Do you know many fishermen that head out after dark?" Reno said.

"She's a sloop," Tredway shouted from the partial forecastle. "Fifty furlongs out and closing."

"This could be good. We're saved," I said.

"This is not the Commonwealth. We have to assume they are pirates," Reno said. "Tredway, do you see any flags?"

"No sir," the lookout shouted.

"To arms!" Reno bellowed. "Get your asses topside and be ready to fight for your meager lives."

"They could be friendly," I said.

"Forty furlongs."

"If they are friendly," Reno said, "then they will understand our caution."

The crew clambered up the ladder onto the main deck, each with a blade or two in hand; seven in all — all save Tomas Flores. He stayed below deck in his cabin.

Each of the crew was sinewy. There wasn't a man among us who hadn't lost a stone or two since the storm. After eleven days of half rations, even I could count my ribs.

Captain Azpa burst through the hatch from his quarters and seemed to climb to the quarterdeck in a single bound.

"Reno to the forecastle," the Captain shouted. The massive former soldier leaped from the quarterdeck and cleared the main deck in the blink of an eye. With the eyepatch over his eye, two spans of beard growth, and the pair of sabers in his belt, the captain cut a fearsome image, like the sailors of legend. "Ferrin, you stay here with me. If they so much as scratch their nose and you did not expect it, you are to burn that ship to the waterline. Understood?"

"Yes sir," I said. My hands shook as I tightened my grip on the splintered tiller.

"Thirty furlongs."

"Breathe deep," Captain Azpa said. "Clear your mind. Focus."

"Ten furlongs."

I took a deep breath of salty air and felt the rocking of the waves. For the first time in what seemed like a span, my mind was clear of everything except the sea and the waves.

"Ho there!" a voice shouted from the other ship as it drew close. An older man stood on the bowsprit of the sloop holding the rigging with the left hand and waving with the right. His skin was as pale. Even after the darkening from the sun, he was paler than anyone I had ever met. The waving man wore a dark woolen shirt and tufts of gray hair poked from under a dark, wide-brimmed hat.

Three other ghost pale men stood on the deck of the small ship amid nets, barrels, and trappings of a fishing vessel.

What a waste of a good, fast ship.

"We saw your ship just before the sun went down," the pale man spoke an older, broken dialect of Imperial through a thick accent.

I've heard that accent before.

"Took you for derelict until we saw lamps after dark. I am Tolek. This is the sloop *Pomsta*. That is Stas, Nik, Ger, and Ewa on stern," Tolek pointed to each of the crew. The last, the navigator, was a slender woman with dark, stringy hair down to her waist.

"We are the merchant cog *Delilah Fritzbink*," Claudio bellowed out in his now raspy Laetian accent. "I am Captain Claudio Azpa. What are your intentions, *Pomsta*?"

The sloop floated a dozen fathoms from the rail of the *Fritzbink*. My eyes darted from one man to the next, looking for any sign of hostility. Each of the pale men stood empty handed though two had knives tucked into their belts. The woman at the helm moved frantically to keep the two vessels close without a collision.

"Food and aid," Tolek said. "Our island is close. Ledeni has a safe harbor for repairs."

Several of the crew looked to the Captain and waited for his response. Claudio exhaled and nodded.

"Well met, *Pomsta*. We could use the help," Claudio shouted. The men let up a cheer and tucked their blades into sashes and scabbards.

"The current is not so strong beyond those rocks," Tolek shouted. "Is your rudder damaged?"

The rocks he pointed to were only quarter furlong off the larboard bow. I pushed the tiller, and the ship glided larboard toward the rocks.

The *Pomsta* moved behind and circled around to our starboard side. As soon as the *Fritzbink* passed out of the current, she slowed and drifted in the dark water. At the captain's order Fawz and Elazaro dropped mooring lines to the smaller ship.

While two of the pale men tied down lines, Kane Cloud, the large Aeromonian sailmaker slid a plank out to the sloop. Tolek climbed the plank, followed by Stas, who carried a bag.

"Permission to come aboard," Tolek said at the top of the plank. The fisherman stood a head taller than the Aeromonian, perhaps eye-level with Reno.

"Granted," Claudio said, hand outstretched to greet the fisherman. "Welcome aboard the *Delilah Fritzbink*, or what is left of her. This is my first mate, Gustavo Blanco, and my master-at-arms, Reno Leon."

Reno and I nodded.

"I heard there were small people in the Dragon Lands," Tolek said. "I never thought I would meet one." He bent low to inspect me closer. At arms distance I could see his hair was not white, but a golden color. His eyes were the same color as the sky, and though wrinkled by the sun, he was much younger than he appeared.

"Gnome. We're called gnomes," I said and shook his massive hand.

"Good to meet you, Lieutenant Blanco," he said before he stood back to his full height. "We have fish, bread, and wine. You all looked half-starved. In morning, we navigate rocks to Ledeni. Tonight, we feast, yes?"

Stas set the sack down. Kane and Tredway took a step back and reached for their blades. Stas held out a hand to ease the sailors, then opened the sack to reveal fresh bread and bottles of wine.

The men of the *Fritzbink* clapped each other on the backs and cheered. It would be the first full meal of fresh food in two spans, perhaps closer to a month.

Two more men soon climbed the plank, each with crates of fresh fish. One had an *oud*-like instrument strapped to his back. Both pale men wore large smiles as they set the food on our deck.

"Niva demands we care for strangers," the youngest fisherman said. He produced a stack of wooden platters and served a fish with the bread.

"Niva? Goddess of winter," I asked as the men huddled around fishermen.

"THE goddess," said the man with the *oud*. His long, dark beard swayed as spoke. "There is only one goddess and we know her as Niva. She is light. She is good."

The fishermen passed out wooden cups to each of the crew and filled each with wine to overflowing.

I motioned to the man with the *oud* and after a moment of hesitation he handed the instrument to me.

It was well-crafted, an instrument too nice for an average fisherman.

I played the first chord of *Drakkan Ladies*, considered our hosts, and changed to the more celebratory *Off Laetian Shores*.

CHAPTER TWENTY-EIGHT

The sun beat down on my face as I awoke. My head throbbed with pain and shoulders ached. I opened my eyes to find I was face down on the deck, my hands and feet bound behind my back. *Those fuckers.*

The sun was high overhead, and I could hear water lapping the side of the ship. *We are moving.* The cry of a gull cut through the silence. *We're close to land.*

I looked around and could see other members of our crew bound and gagged on the deck near me. Most looked bound with hempen line, though Reno wore iron manacles around his wrists.

"The small one stirs," the graveled voice of the bearded pirate said somewhere behind my back.

"Pick him up," Tolek said.

I felt a pair of hands grab me, lift me off the deck, and place me down on my knees. Claudio was bound beside me, a dark bruise formed on his face, and dried blood ran down from his mouth and stained the deck.

Tredway lay in a heap at the base of the ladder near the forecastle. He was on watch last night and had forgone the wine. His throat was slit, and the crimson pooled around his body.

"Lieutenant Blanco," Tolek said. "Tell me, what treasures are the Drakkans transporting this far north?"

"Fuck you."

A hand gripped my hair. The bearded pirate stepped around from behind and drove a punch into my stomach. Doubled over with the pain, I concentrated on the waves. I would need to heal myself.

"Forgive me," Tolek said, his demeanor calm, cold even. "My Imperial is out of practice. What cargo do you carry on your ship?"

"Chisels so we can break off the ice to get at your mother's frozen cunny," I said. I waited for the hand to grab my hair again, but it never came. Instead a massive boot connected with my jaw, and my vision went black.

I came to again as my body was thrown against something hard and metallic. My jaw hurt and my left eye was swollen shut. I tried to concentrate on the sea, a desperate attempt to build my *yili*. Nothing. I couldn't hear the waves or feel the rocking of the ship. It was dark. I was in a cage. Somewhere.

I sat motionless, my body rocked as though it missed the sea. I set my *sebi* inward, took my own *yili* and focused it on my wounds. With a word, the swelling subsided, and I could see. Another and my jaw set with a flash of excruciating pain. My hands still tied behind my back.

The cage was a tight cube, my height in any direction. It was inside a cramped wooden structure, a shed or a shanty. The tight space filled with a foul stench. Nothing moved — the walls, the floor — it was an odd sensation. *I must be on land, their island perhaps?* It was strange how uncomfortable I felt on land after a little more than a month at sea.

My eyes soon adjusted to the darkness, and I discovered the source of the stench — a corpse in the next cage over. I craned my head to get a better look at his face. He was not one of the crew. *Why capture us? Why not kill us at sea?*

I shifted my weight and brought my arms in front me. It sure as hell wasn't the first time someone had left me bound and alone. *At least this time I still had my clothes.* I used my teeth to pull apart the knot and release my hands, then my feet, and rubbed at the marks on my wrists.

I closed my eyes and tried to search for sources of energy as I had done before on the ship. One by one the threads of the Fabric revealed themselves. I could see the cage and the shack. The threads ran to the body in the cage next to mine. Where the crew each had a glow of the *yili* within them, however faint, this man had no light within him. He was dead.

I scanned the threads further. To my surprise I found I could see beyond the walls through the threads, at least six or seven fathoms out. Some threads revealed other sources of life, men — pirates — walked around the camp. There were several other small shacks in a line. Within each was a huddled group of three to four people. *How many captives did they have? We aren't the only ship they've come across, if this man is any sign.*

A fire burned only a few fathoms from a line of shacks. Three men stood near the fire, huddled together. Their *yili* glowed with the same golden energy as those in the shacks. I could make out their forms but could not see what they were doing.

We're in some encampment. The door-latch on the shanty shifted, and my vision raced back into the material world as I jumped in terror.

The sky outside was dark. *Had it been a day since the pirates approached?* A dark figure stood in the doorway, silhouetted by the fire. As they stepped into the shack, I could tell that it was an older woman. She was pale skinned, like the pirates. She wore dark furs, her long, gray hair matted and dirty. She carried two bowls of stew. The stench of the bowls overpowered the putrid scent of the dead man.

"Who are you?" I asked as the woman set the bowls down on a table and picked up an iron bar.

"What are you doing with that?" I shouted as the woman moved toward the cages. She prodded the dead man with the iron bar and frowned.

"He's dead," I said. "Your people killed him."

The woman pointed at me with the iron bar. My face pressed against the bars as I shouted at her. "Where are my friends? Have you killed them too?"

She pointed at me again and made a swatting motion with her free hand. I took a step from the bars, and she grabbed a bowl from the table and slid it into the cage. The smell of rotted fish assaulted my nostrils. The woman mimed eating and pointed to the bowl then turned to leave.

"Please," I begged. "Don't leave me in here with him." She may not understand my words, but she could understand the tone. I pointed to the corpse in the next cage.

The woman nodded as she stepped through the door and closed it behind her. Once again, I was alone in darkness with the smell of a corpse, and now rancid fish stew.

* * *

A few marks after the woman left, the door to the shack slammed open again. The door flew back with such force the cage shook, spilling rancid fish stew on the wood slats of the floor. A large man stood in the door, his wild hair glowed in the fire behind him like a terrible aura. He wielded an iron bar like the one the woman had used.

The man thrashed the bar against my cage and said something in a language I couldn't understand. I pressed myself against the back of the cage, my eyes wide. With a laugh, he moved to the cage with the corpse and prodded the body with the iron bar. The bar pierced the chest of the dead man with a sickening sound. The large man gagged in disgust, looked over his shoulder, and shouted out the door.

A moment later a second, younger man entered the shanty. The younger man winced as the stench hit him. The larger man pointed to the body and said something to the younger. They grabbed the body, iron bar still protruding from his chest, and carried him from the shack.

For a moment I could see through the door. I tried to commit as much of the scene to memory: two women and a man next to a bonfire, a row of wooden shacks across the fire from my own, a group of ramshackle houses on a rise.

The large man returned and slammed closed the shanty door. The putrid stew spilled on the floor boards once again, a welcome cover to the morbid aroma.

My thread visions had been right. There was a fire beyond the door with people huddled around it. If that was true, then perhaps the people in the other shacks were real too. The rest of the crew may still be alive.

Comforted by the thought my friends may be safe, if trapped in a cage, I leaned against the cold bars and considered my options.

CHAPTER TWENTY-NINE

In my fifth year of formal study at the Imperial University, Ignis allowed me to leave campus when I wasn't in classes. I often found myself in one of the many public houses just beyond the walls of the campus, gathering the latest gossip from the older students with my midday meal.

I had nestled into a booth away from the crowded bar, captivated by a history of Fadlan's travels.

The shadows of the dim room and the general apathy of the barkeep at this establishment would, in a few years, make it easier for a gnome of twelve years to order a tankard of ale with my older classmates. For the time I settled for a platter of figs, goat cheese, and the relative peace of the back booth.

Fadlan, renowned as the first Drakkan to travel the remains of the Eisig Empire after the Azurean Wars, had just reached the continent of Nivalis and was recounting his horror with the sanitary habits of the Eisiger people. A young boy almost tall enough to look over the table, with shaggy black hair, stood at the end of the booth staring at me. I tried to shift and ignore the dirty-faced child.

"I don't have any money to give you," I said. It was the truth. Shari, the owner of the public house, was a client of the Empire. She offered food, drink, and a place to sleep for a reduced price when Zori's men came with the monthly invoices.

"Don't want your money," the boy said. "I work for my own."

I returned to my book. He continued to stare.

"Why are you staring? Go away," I said.

"Never saw a small man before," he said. "Can I draw you?"

"Gnome," I corrected. "Can you do it without bothering me?"

"Sure. It'll cost you." He sat on the bench across the table from me and pulled a piece of paper and a box of charcoal from a satchel he wore across his chest.

"I thought you didn't want my money?"

"Don't want your charity. But I'll take your money for work. Copper half knot for a sketch."

I laughed. A child no older than me, and he had already perfected his hustle. I reached into the coin purse tucked inside my tunic, felt for a half knot, and handed it to him.

He palmed the coin and it disappeared to somewhere on his filthy person. He opened his box of charcoal and marked the paper. Content he would stay quiet, I returned to Fadlan's horror at Eisiger's tendency to bathe only once a month.

A few moments later the child slid the paper across the table for my inspection. The portrait was a striking likeness of me slumped over my book.

"This is really good," I said.

"Thank you," he said. "Name's Dem." He flagged down Shari as she moved between the tables in the front and the kitchen in the back.

"I already told you. If you don't have money, you get no food. I'm not a Panean," Shari said with indignation. "And get out that boy's booth. You leave him alone."

Dem held up the tarnished half knot he received. "Can I get that stew now?"

"Are you hustling my patrons?"

"It's alright," I said.

Shari studied the filthy boy through narrow eyes for a moment, then plucked the copper piece from his tiny hand and headed to the kitchen.

"I'm surprised that you can read," he said.

"Of course I can. Can't you?" I asked.

"Nah, that's one of those things for rich people and the smart folk behind the walls of their school," he said. "I don't have much need for it. So which are you?"

My face must have conveyed the confusion. Shari arrived and placed down a steaming bowl of goat stew and half a loaf of warm bread in front of the filthy child.

"Are you smart? Or rich?" he asked.

"Both," Shari said.

I shot a cold glance at the tavern keeper. She shrugged her shoulders, picked up an empty coffee cup from the table, and headed back toward the kitchen.

Dem nodded a grunt of approval. Her answer seemed to satisfy his question. He ladled a spoonful of the stew into his mouth.

"So what are you reading?" He asked between bites of bread.

"History of Fadlan's first journey," I said in a tone I hoped conveyed my disinterest in further conversation.

"Who's that?"

"A man who sailed north a long time ago."

"I heard there were nothing but bad people in the north. They eat people."

I snorted. "They aren't all bad people. And they aren't cannibals."

Dem munched on a chunk of bread while he considered his next question.

"So what do you study at the school behind the wall?"

I closed my book, convinced I wouldn't be able to read any further. "Mostly about dead people. Sometimes we get to read about dead animals too. If we're lucky, we get to read about dead civilizations."

"The priests say too much fascination with the dead is a dangerous thing, especially when the people with the books do it," he said.

"It's important to know what others have already learned. Otherwise we would go nowhere as a society," I said. "Are you actually comparing the study of history with necromancy?"

"Necro-what? The priests just say fiddling with dead things is bad."

I let out an exhausted sigh.

"Yeah, a lot of people say that I can be tiring. I can leave if you want."

"No, finish your meal."

By the time we had both finished our food and left the tavern for the evening the sky was already dark. It was the first time I had to climb over the great walls of the college in the dead of night, but it wasn't the last. From that day when I was eight-years-old, Dem and I were inseparable.

CHAPTER THIRTY

I t was still dark in the shanty. The cold, damp air carried the smell of a fire over the putrid smell that still permeated the shanty. The bolt on the door shifted, and the door opened.

Beyond the door, the encampment was dark. Fires glowed both here in the slave camp and in the shantytown on the rise. *Is that what we are, slaves?*

The old woman who brought the bowl of rotten fish stew the night before entered. She carried her iron bar in her left hand—retrieved from the corpse dragged out last night—and a wooden platter with a slice of bread and a charred fish. Once again, she swatted at me with her bar, and I pressed my back against the far side of the cage.

"What time is it? What day?" I asked.

She ignored my questions and slipped the platter between the bars of my cage. *How long had it been since I had actual bread instead of hardtack?* As she stepped back from my cage, I attacked the bread. She watched me with curiosity. The bread was stale, but better than the fish stew that still lingered in the air. I picked at the charred fish, it was a type I couldn't recognize. The sweet meat was still warm if lacking in spices.

Satisfied I was eating, the woman stepped out of the shanty and closed the door behind her.

* * *

I tried my best to move about and stretch my aching muscles. Several turns after the morning meal it was still dark. I remembered hearing stories of lands in the far north of Nivalis where the sun would not rise for months at a time. *But we aren't that far north…are we?*

The bolt on the door shifted, and the door opened. I expected the woman to bring a midday meal, but instead found Tolek, the pirate captain, at the door.

"Your wounds are healing well," he said in his accented Imperial.

"Is my captain still alive?"

"Everyone is still alive."

"Not everyone," I said as visions flooded my mind of Tredway's body, throat slashed and bleeding on the deck of the *Fritzbink*. The air still heavy with the stench of death only amplified the memories for me.

"Your captain is still alive," he said.

"So go talk to him."

"Ger is…" he paused, selected his words with care. "Persuading him to talk. I wanted to speak to you."

"There is nothing I can tell you, I was an apprentice until the day you found us. I hadn't been first mate three turns before we spotted your sails on the horizon."

He laughed but didn't take his eyes off me. "What can you tell me about your cargo?"

"Why are you so obsessed with the cargo? It's farming equipment headed to an outer island," I said.

Tolek roared with laughter. "It would take months to plow a field with these."

He pulled a shining sword from a scabbard at his waist and threw it on the floor in front of my cage.

I sat and stared at the blade. It was new, not a blemish on it. It bore the markings of a Drakkan smiths guild.

"Your surprise is genuine," Tolek said. "You honestly didn't know you had a hold full of weapons?" He hefted the blade and slid it back into its sheath, then leaned against the table.

"Like I said, I was an apprentice, a midshipman on a merchant ship," I said. "Until a few days ago I was studying charts and attempting to tell my starboard from larboard. When the first mate died following the storm, the captain appointed me as first mate."

"But if you are as green as you claim, why promote you?"

"Because I was the only one who survived," I said. The painful truth hung in the shanty's silence with the smell of death and rancid fish stew.

Tolek gave a hearty laugh, "In my culture, the one who survived is the one to be feared. You are a tiny man in a tiny cage though. Should I fear you, Lieutenant Blanco?"

Lost in my thoughts, I stared at the wooden slats of my prison.

"There is nothing to fear here," Tolek said as he stood and moved toward the door. "Only a broken, small man."

CHAPTER THIRTY-ONE

I n the turns of solitude inside my prison I focused my attention on the lock of the cage. With the threads I could see the mechanism of the lock, the tumbler, the pins. For what seemed like days of concentration I set my *sebi* on the lock and demanded my *agoti* to move the lock.

There is a school of magic dedicated to the ability of an arcanist to move the objects with their *agoti*. When I was still a student in the University, I used to watch the Kinetimancers practice. They crafted enormous granite towers in the University's courtyard without ever touching the stones.

In the darkness of my cage I searched my memory of the Ancient Tongue, the words many arcanist uses to manipulate the Fabric. I tried the arcane words for turn, break, yield. None seemed to work, though a cockroach surrendered, tiny arms raised in capitulation before it scurried away.

When arcane means failed, I moved to more mundane methods. Viewed through the Threads I maneuvered a spoon, slick with the oily fish stew, through the wide keyhole to the pins. I twisted the spoon left, then right, then with a final twist, *CLICK*.

My heart leaped in my chest with the sound. The door to the cage slid open with only a faint sound. My excitement overwhelmed my *sebi* and my sight again filled with the decrepit shack, this time from the other side of the cage.

I need to plan this with care. If I rush this, it won't end well for me. I stepped back into my cage, careful to lock the door behind. I waited.

* * *

That night after the old woman brought a fresh bowl of rancid fish stew, I watched the camp through the threads. Thin fibers of reality stretched out in all directions, taking the shapes of structures and people. It was several turns before the movement in the camp slowed as my captors turned in for the night.

With deft skill I crammed my spoon-turned-lock pick into the tumbler and once again I was free. I moved to the door of my wooden prison, spoon in hand, slid the bolt, and opened the door.

High cliffs surrounded the encampment on three sides. *Not cliffs, walls. That explains the constant darkness.* They built the camp, a small village of ramshackle buildings, on a rise inside a massive cave. Ten wooden shanties made a halfmoon around a large bonfire on a lower level of the cave.

I slipped around the side of my prison and into the dark shadows cast along the cave walls. In the dark I skulked to the next shanty where I could still sense three men in cages.

Only two of the pale-skinned pirates watched the shanties after the evening meal. One had fiery red hair, the other light gold. Both wore furs over their clothes. The two engaged in a heated debate in their strange language. While the guards argued, I moved to the front of the shanty, pulled aside the latch, and entered.

Inside the air was thick with the scent of sweat and feces. The smell made me gag.

"Who is there?" A voice said from one cage.

"It is Fer—Lieutenant Blanco," Jabnit replied.

As my eyes adjusted the darkness once again, I could see three men crammed into the same small cages they used to hold me. In one was Jabnit. Another held Majid Al Din Din, the ship's cook, and the third held a man I didn't recognize.

"Blanco? Who is Blanco?" Majid asked.

It was then it occurred to me that humans had difficulty seeing in the dark.

"It's me, Majid," I said. "We need to get out. Do you know where the others are?"

"I'm not sure," he replied. "How did you know we were here?"

230

"It was the first shanty next to mine," I said.

I slid my spoon into the lock on the cook's cage. As the lock clicked open, the unknown man pleaded with me, "Take me with you. Don't leave me here. I've been in this cage for three spans."

No sooner was the cook's cage open did I see Jabnit's cage ajar.

"Did you—"

"Yes."

"You have picks on you?"

"Always," Jabnit said as he climbed out of his cage. "You do not?"

I held up the spoon, and he nodded. "What do we do with him?"

"We need crewmen," Jabnit said.

"I'm an able sailor," the man in the cage said.

I turned to the third cage and popped the lock open. The sailor crawled from his cage. "Thank you. Gods have mercy on you, Blanco."

"There are two men at a fire in the center of a ring of shanties like this one," I said. The three men were all hunched, their faces winced as they stretched and attempted to stand upright. "Stay to the shadows behind shanties."

Jabnit and the others followed me behind the wooden prison which once held them. Once we were in the shadows Jabnit leaned forward and whispered.

"What is this darkness they talk about?" Jabnit asked.

"Who?"

"The guards," Jabnit said. "They speak of being attacked by the darkness again. They are afraid Tolek has led them to their deaths."

"You can speak Niv?" I asked.

"Eisiger," he said. "I can. You do not?"

"No," I said. "I can only speak Imperial."

"How do you plan to be a sailor if you can only speak one language?" Jabnit asked.

"What are you talking about?" I asked.

"So many ports, so many languages along the Azurean Sea coast." he said.

"Not that," I said. "About the darkness? What did you say?"

"They speak of the darkness," he said. "I do not understand. Does this have another meaning? Have you ever heard of it?"

Darkness? It sounds familiar. I've heard of it somewhere. Where I had heard their accent before? Dem spoke of the darkness. Didn't he? Some tale the Ice Eaters tell each other.

"They fear their dead," I said, "say the darkness can make them walk. It's just an Ice Eater ghost story."

"Nivaleans," he corrected again. "This darkness, it terrifies them. It seems strange that they would hide in the ground if they were so afraid of it."

"We can worry about their housing choices later," I said. "Do you know where Reno is being held?"

"They forced him into the shack next to ours," Majid said. "I was awake when they brought us here. They did not know."

"You said you didn't know where anyone was." I said. "That shack?"

I pointed who the next Shanty in the line.

"I said I was not sure," Majid said. "Seeing it now, I'm certain. It took four men to drag him in there."

"Right then," I said. "You three wait here I'll be back in a moment."

I stuck my head around the corner of the shanty. The two guards still argued with each other. I ran the short distance to the next shed and rolled behind, out of their view. Waiting just long enough to catch my breath, I snuck around the side of the wooden structure and opened the latch to Reno's prison.

"Already back for more?" Reno said in his graveled voice.

They forced Reno onto his knees and chained him at the neck, wrist, waist, and feet to the walls of the shanty and two heavy stones on the floor.

"Yeah, I was hoping for a lot more," I said with a chuckle.

His shoulders slumped.

"Ferrin is that you?" he said. "What are you doing here? How did you escape?"

I held up my trusty spoon. Reno just laughed.

"So I take it you have not learned the command word to unlock these chains?"

I looked at the locks binding Reno to the shanty wall. There was no way I could fit the spoon into the smaller keyholes of these locks.

"No," I said. "I spent turns guessing."

Reno chuckled, "Had I known we would have been in this situation, I would have taught you that first. Do you have a source for your *yili* here?"

"Yes, a large bonfire a short distance outside the door of this shack. It provides a great source."

Reno closed his eyes, gathering the *yili* within him. When he was ready, he spoke two arcane words: *iron* and *yield*.

With all the strength he could muster, he pulled, and the chain which bound his wrists to the wall snapped free. He rubbed at his wrists, then with his free hands he grabbed the steel collar and ripped it from his neck. The thick iron chains yielded to his command. As he stood, the chains on his waist and his legs broke free.

"You must use the true name of the object you wish to control," he said. "Otherwise, it will not know you speak to it."

I nodded in understanding.

"Why didn't you do that before?"

"I thought I was alone. I am too weak to take them on by myself. I thought I would gather my strength and fight when I was strong enough."

"Please don't tell me you ate the rancid fish stew."

"It was good."

Reno reached over my head to an iron bar, like the one in my prison and gave it an appraising flex. He nodded in approval.

"So, is it you and me?" he asked.

"Jabnit, Majid, and someone else are waiting behind a shack just outside."

"How many guards?"

"Only two watching us," I said. "And they are deep in conversation."

"Well, I would hate to interrupt a good conversation," Reno said with a smile.

Iron bar in hand, Reno kicked open the door to his prison. I saw the two guards jump as the door slammed against the wooden wall.

Reno had crossed half the distance to the bonfire before the guards recognized what was happening. He spoke another arcane word, this time for *silence*. It seemed nothing happened, but I could no longer hear the commotion on the other side of the bonfire. At that same time Jabnit and Majid ran behind the guards. With the strength that comes from years on the sea the two sailors snapped the necks of the pale-skinned guards.

I pointed to Reno and said, "We need to find the captain."

Jabnit and Majid carried the bodies of the two guards into the shanty that had been their prison.

The other sailor took a lookout position near the line of shanties.

I ran to the next shed in the line and pulled the door open. I recognized none of the five in cages in this room, but I knew they would be of help to us as we tried to mount an escape. Closing my eyes, I focused on drawing in the *yili* of the fire.

As soon as I had the energy, I set my *sebi* on the iron cages and used the commands Reno taught me: *iron yield*.

As I grabbed the cage door, the metal disintegrated in my hand. I pulled on each of the other doors, and, like the first, each yielded in my grasp. In moments the five captive sailors, three men and two women, crawled free of their cages and made for the door.

I pushed past them and ran to the next shed, still searching for the Captain.

In the next shack I found the sailmaker Kane Cloud along with the two carpenters from the *Fritzbink*. Using the same command I ripped free the cage doors and helped them to their feet.

"Do any of you know where the captain is being held?" I asked.

"No," Kane said. "I woke up in this tiny cage and have been here for days."

"Ferrin," Reno had stuck his head into the door with a frantic look on his face. "I need you to come with me. I found the captain. He is…"

I rushed out of the wooden shack and followed Reno. A group of freed sailors stood near the bonfire.

"Set up a defensive perimeter! Don't just stand around," I commanded them.

Reno led me to a shack three down from where he found me. The door was already ajar. As my eyes adjusted to the dark interior of the shanty, I could see Captain Azpa bloodied on the floor inside a small cage.

"Open the cage already," I said to Reno.

Without objection Reno spoke the two words and ripped the cage in two. I climbed inside with the captain, pulling the energy from the fire into my well. I set my *sebi* on the captain and recited the arcane words to heal his most severe wounds.

I looked through the threads at the captain. I could see he had suffered a severe beating. Had we not found him when we did, I doubt he would have survived the night.

*　*　*

It took the better part of a turn before the captain regained consciousness. I had never used that much *yili* to heal a single person. Something tells me Tomas would not have approved.

Claudio coughed as I helped him to a seated position.

"Ferrin, you need to find Tomas," the captain said, his voice a coarse whisper. "No matter your feelings for him, he is one of us."

I looked to Reno.

"We have not seen him," he said.

"Tolek and the others took him to their village when they found out he could heal their injured," Claudio said.

"You want us to go into their village?" I asked. "It will be swarming with pirates. If we leave now, there's a chance we could escape, all of us, even the ones we found. If we go on the search for Tomas, there's no chance we get out of here alive."

"That was not a request, Lieutenant Alsahar," Claudio said. "He is a Drakkan, just like you. If the roles were reversed, he would be out looking for you."

"Understood, Captain," I said. "Reno, stay here and work on getting the rest of these sailors free from their cages. If I'm not back before the new watch arrives, flee without us."

"Yes, Lieutenant."

If my observations were correct, the watch changed three times every day. That would mean a new watch would arrive eight turns after the last one.

Counting the time from the last watch's arrival to the time the camp fell still for the night, the time we took to free the captive sailors, and the full turn I needed to heal the captain's wounds, it would be perhaps two turns before the next watch arrived at the prison camp.

That would be two turns to explore the village on the rise, locate the doctor, free him from whatever bonds he found himself in, and return to the prison camp to attempt our escape. *If I was right, I have two turns. Arkanus help me, I hope I'm right.* I tucked my spoon into my sash and trudged up the embankment to the village.

CHAPTER THIRTY-TWO

The narrow, haphazard paths between shanty houses conjured memories of being chased through Smugglers Scourge the night I fled Drakkas Port. Small fires burned in the larger intersections and bathed the main thoroughfares — if any of these footpaths could be thoroughfares — in light and cast deep shadows on the side alleys. It was to the darker paths I moved, hoping to conceal my presence for as long as possible.

In my mind it was a certainty they would spot me. I knew at any moment a pirate stumbling into a back alley to relieve himself would find a spoon-wielding gnome arcanist skulking behind his latrine and in a desperate attempt to defend myself I would touch off a fevered battle between a band of sailors turned slaves and an army of ruthless pirates.

What in the ten hells am I doing here? I'm no soldier. Gnomes don't do things like this.

The village already proved to be larger than I first thought. I passed the tenth row of rough built structures and could see countless more. They constructed the buildings out of pieces of shipwrecks and other detritus which must have washed ashore on the island. The cave provided shelter from the elements, so many of the roofs were little more than sail canvas. *So many opportunities to be heard.*

A few blocks further, the path I followed into the heart of the village opened onto a small plaza. I halfway expected to find cobbles and a fountain in the center. Instead I discovered a pile of crates that bore the markings of the Southern Empire Trading Company — the cargo of the *Delilah Fritzbink*.

Several of the crates were pried open, their contents on display. One crate stamped "plows," held a dozen bright blades of the kind Tolek had shown me in my cage. Another marked "bridles and bits," contained five heavy crossbows and as many satchels of bolts. "Saddles" proved to be boiled leather cuirasses, enough to outfit an entire column. In a final open crate I discovered the "spade heads" were daggers. I grabbed two blades as long as my arm and tucked them into my sash along with my spoon.

If the crates are here, Tolek must be nearby, and perhaps Tomas.

The sound of footfalls reverberated off the cave walls. Someone was running through the paths of the shanty village.

I sunk low into an empty crate of "saddles" as the footsteps grew closer. A young man with golden hair and the same furs of the other guards burst onto the plaza from the dim thoroughfare. He doubled over and grabbed his knees breathing hard. He inhaled deep as though he was about to shout.

I closed my eyes and pulled *yili* from the nearest street fire a block away. It wasn't strong, but it would have to do. I set my *sebi* on the pirate and said the arcane word Reno had used at the campfire. The golden-haired man's face contorted as his shouts did not come. His eyes widened as I leapt from my hiding spot and charged at him.

Step. Step. Silence.

Dagger drawn, I closed the distance between us in two heartbeats. The Drakkan blade flashed with the dim golden light of a nearby fire as it tore through the furs and the leathers hidden underneath. It sunk deep into his chest. Pulsed in time with his pounding heart. Then splashed crimson across the cold gray stone as the dagger pulled free. The pirate collapsed into a silent pile at my feet.

I killed him.

There was no time for remorse. His death meant I was still alive. I grabbed the feet of the man and pulled him into a dark side path and covered the pool of blood with a canvas.

I surveyed the plaza. One shanty was larger than the surrounding structures. *This must be Tolek's place.*

The door into the shanty was the top to a crate. As I pulled the door open, I could see the first room had a large table in the center with nautical charts of the northern Azurean Sea along with the shipping manifests of a dozen vessels.

The interior rooms had no doors, which allowed me to survey each from the connecting hallway. Most rooms were sleeping quarters, with thick piles of furs on the floor, men and women intertwined atop them.

I stepped into the last room at the end of the hallway. A man, naked from the waist up, stood in the doorway with his face twisted in confusion. Not any man: Tolek. The pale man inhaled deeply, surprised to find I wasn't a dream.

My crimson blade already drawn, I leapt up and pulled it across his neck. Tolek grabbed his throat as he fell to his knees. He struggled to shout, but a gurgled whisper was all he could produce as the blood seeped from his opened neck and mouth. I placed both hands on the pommel of the dagger and drove the blade through his skull.

The body collapsed to the floor.

Behind the crumpled torturer I saw the horrified face of Tomas as he sat in an upholstered chair. One hand held a book, the other covered his mouth.

"This is how you live as your crew is being locked in cages and beaten to death?" My voice was a whisper but carried the fury of a squall.

"I was working to get you all released," he said.

"Claudio would have been dead by morning, and you are up here gorging yourself on looted goods," I struggled to keep my voice down and was at risk of alerting the entire encampment to my location. "Are you bound?"

"No," he said.

"Good. We are leaving. Follow my directions and move swift and silent," I said and turned toward the hallway. I jumped over the body of Tolek and led Tomas down the hall, through the chart room and out into the plaza. We snaked through the back streets toward the slave camp. The doctor kept pace as I hurried back to our crew.

As I reached the embankment that led down to the crescent of wooden shacks, shouts of alarm rose from the village. Twenty-five sailors in the slave camp below looked at Tomas and I as we ran down toward them and out of the cave.

"We must go. Now!" Captain Azpa shouted.

All the former captives turned and ran with the order. The caves wound around several times before the bright light of the morning sun appeared at the entrance of the caves.

CHAPTER THIRTY-THREE

We each ran as hard as we could. Even the portly Doctor Flores proved nimble when the situation required it. My eyes struggled to adjust to the light as we reached the mouth of the caves. I stumbled over a stone and tumbled, face first, into the gravel. A quick roll protected my face from the stones, and the massive hand of Reno reached down, grabbed hold of the torn collar of my shirt, and jerked me back to my feet in a fluid motion.

As my eyes focused, I glimpsed the silhouette of the abomination that the *Fritzbink* had become anchored in the harbor. Aside from the sorry state of the storm-wrecked ship, thick spars, little more than tree trunks with the branches lopped off, jutted from the ship both fore and aft.

The spars joined to the *Pomsta*, creating a crude outrigger, which used the sails the smaller vessel to bring our craft to the pirates' harbor.

The lot of us, twenty-seven in all, exploded through the cave opening and raced toward the waterline.

"What did they do to my ship?" said one captive, a Drakkan woman with long hair pulled back into a tail, her mouth agape at the sight of the outrigger monstrosity.

"Worry later," Captain Azpa said. "Get to the shore boats."

A volley of bolts rained down on the beach. I looked over my shoulder, and I could see the Nivaleans press the nose of their weapons into the ground and pull back the string to prepare another round.

"Arbalists in the cave opening!" I shouted.

"No shit."

"Ferrin, keep them distracted."

"With what? A jaunty tune?"

"*Sebi. Yili. Agoti,*" Reno bellowed as he lifted a shore boat over his head. The oars dangled from the oarlocks like a petulant animal kicking to get free.

I stopped short of the line of row boats, took a deep breath, and closed my eyes. The chaos of the surrounding skirmish slowed. Even with my eyes closed tight I could see the whole field as the threads lay out before me. I set my *sebi* on the band of pirates using boulders at the mouth of the caves for defense.

In a single heartbeat I could feel the energy surge through my body. Another heartbeat. The energy popped as the Fabric thrummed with anticipation. Flames licked at my fingertips even as the thought of what attack to use solidified in my mind. A third heartbeat. I took a step forward toward the Nivaleans. A single word passed my lips. The arcane word thundered along the cliff face as though Cassis himself had barked the order.

The threads vibrated out from me to the area I had chosen, an unprotected spot just above the boulders. A wave of white-hot flames rippled into existence above the pirate archers and consumed them in fire.

As I released my *sebi*, the world around me rushed back to a normal speed. My head spun as reality snapped my eyes open.

Cries of agony from the burning Nivaleans reverberated off the cave walls and amplified their pleas of mercy to their goddess. *I had caused this suffering.*

I turned to run toward the boat as a pirate leaped over a stone outcropping, sword drawn and dove toward me. I brandished my dagger and entered the Torchbearer stance, my arm outstretched. Spans of training allowed me to react without thought. My blade swiped out across the man's chest. Blood seeped from his wound as he tumbled to the ground, rolled, and jumped back to his feet. I shifted to Greedy Goblin.

I concentrated again on the chaos of the beach, and the world slowed once more. The pirate prepared to charge again. I set my *sebi* on the man's wound, the blood poured from his chest. I clenched my fist as though I had grabbed his shirt and was about to throw him. I joined the arcane words I had learned to heal and those to control the raw power of the elements shouted out *blood yield*, and pulled my fist away with all my might.

At once the blood of the pirate ripped through his chest and formed the outline of the man in front of him. His face contorted to the look of horror before he crumpled into the sand.

All around the beach, people collapsed to the ground as their sanguine apparitions appeared before them.

Oh gods, what have I done?

I unclenched my hand. A crimson rain fell on the golden sands of Ledeni.

The rescued sailors stood in horrified silence as waves lapped the shore.

No one moved. Not the Nivaleans. Not the sailors.

What have I done?

The remaining *Fritzbink* crew grabbed the stunned sailors and threw them into the awaiting boats.

I jumped into a shore boat with Reno, and the hulking brute rowed with every muscle in his body.

We reached the *Pomsta* and scurried up a ladder onto the deck of the sloop. Claudio and Jabnit leaped onto the bow outrigger beam and climbed on the deck of the *Fritzbink*. Rescued sailors took to the rigging and readied the sails. A second later, a

Nivalean flew over the rail of the ship. A crimson tail flowing from a gaping neck wound followed.

"We have the ship!" Claudio bellowed from the deck above. "Mister Jabnit, bring us about. Lieutenant Alsahar, we could use wind."

The Drakkan with the long hair ran to the tiller of the *Pomsta* to aid in the maneuvers. I closed my eyes and could once again feel the sway of the sea — not sway, shove. Reno had grabbed hold of the Fabric of the sea itself and used it to shove the ship about.

I set my *sebi* on the limp canvas of the *Pomsta* and spoke the word for wind. The oversized canvas filled as I spoke the word again. The jury-rigged ships heaved forward as the *Pomsta's* sail pulled the two through the water.

Claudio stood along the rail of the *Fritzbink's* quarterdeck and shouted orders to both helmsmen as the ships navigated the shoal and into deeper water.

* * *

As the sun reached the horizon astern, the ships slid into the Azurean Currents. I felt the pull of the sea on the hulls and released my *sebi*.

"I've never seen a mage keep focus for so long," the Drakkan helmsman said as I sat on the deck next to the tiller.

"The ladies of Drakkas Port have helped me with my stamina," I said. I laughed, then realized she was not amused.

"It's no wonder the price on your head is so high," she said.

Chills struck me as I struggled to comprehend her words through the exhaustion. I stared for a long moment at the woman. *How was it possible? She could have left Drakkas Port only a day or two after the Fritzbink and to get picked up by the pirates before us.*

"You heard about me in Drakkas Port?"

She shook her head. "Whyte Harbor. Soldiers swarmed the port asking before we left. Fifty gold ships for the capture of the murderer and traitor Ferrin Alsahar. They even had a dragon with them, perched atop the Whyte Citadel like a gull on a piece of driftwood."

"Fifty?" I choked on the words. Fifty ships was more than even a skilled captain would make in ten lifetimes. *Who could afford a bounty that high?*

"As Res as my witness, I will not speak a word of this. None of my crew will," the Drakkan woman said in a solemn tone. "You saved us all today. We — I owe you a blood debt."

She held her right hand to her heart and nodded.

"Well, fuck," I said.

CHAPTER THIRTY-FOUR

"Ho, *Pomsta*!" Lurco, the ship's carpenter, shouted from the rail of the *Fritzbink*. "Cap'n wants all officers in the Fritz's mess in two marks."

"They called you Lieutenant didn't they, Master Alsahar?" the Drakkan woman asked.

"They did," I said. "And, I want to say, Captain…"

"Najat Kalb," she said with a smirk. "Captain of the sloop *Pomsta*, Drakkan Trading Company."

"Ah, the proprietor is a friend of mine," I said.

"So I have heard," Captain Najat said, her eyes narrowed.

Lurco threw a sheet down to a sailor on the deck of the *Pomsta*. The sailor hauled the sheet in, then pulled the damaged shroud of the *Fritzbink* across the gap between the two ships. The ladder-like structure created a means to cross between the two vessels. After the sailor fastened the shroud, Lurco wrestled a piece of timber over the rail to use as a gangplank.

The sailor looked to Najat, "Ready for you, Captain." The deckhand's eyes widened as he recognized me standing at her side. He placed his fist over his heart as Najat had done and nodded.

"After you," Captain Najat said with a flourish.

"Permission to come aboard," I shouted to Lurco as I stepped onto the gangplank.

"Granted, Lieutenant, welcome aboard," the carpenter said.

"Captain Kalb of the *Pomsta*," Najat announced. "Permission to come aboard."

"Aye, Captain, welcome." Lurco looked to me, "I didn't realize I was on watch."

A lean Laetian man climbed down from the rigging and approached the gangplank. His voice was smooth and dry, "Ensign Orlan Barrera of the *Azurean Strela*."

"Welcome, Ensign," the carpenter said. "Right, any other officers?"

"Did Captain Azpa say why he needed us all, Lurco?" I asked as I waited for any final officers on the smaller ship.

A tall Aeromonian woman waved from the bow of the *Pomsta*. "I'm an officer."

"Cap'n wants ye in the mess, ma'am. Hurry," Lurco shouted, then looked to me. "Didn't say, but I s'pose he wants to decide our next move."

I nodded as the tall woman walked to the end the gang plank.

"Lieutenant Elia Cloud, Quartermaster of the *Kestrel's Wing*," she said.

"*Kestrel's Wing*? That's an Empire ship," I said.

"Aye, it is," she said, then corrected herself with a frown. "Was."

"Welcome aboard the *Fritzbink*, Lieutenant," Lurco said.

"Ellie?" a voice shouted from the hatch of the *Pomsta* as the quartermaster cleared the rail of the larger ship. The towering sailmaker Kane Cloud held a bundle of canvas in his arms as he looked to the crossing officer.

"Kane!" she said. "Wait there, I'll be back in a few."

"You know our sailmaker?" Lurco asked.

"Vaguely," she said as she walked toward the officers' mess. "He's my baby brother."

* * *

"We just do not have the food for a voyage to Lesser Auster," Reno said to the gathered group huddled in the mess. "Even on quarter rations, we will run out before we reach the outer islands."

"Why not trim the sails and set a course toward Whyte Harbor? We take refuge at night in the leeward side of these islands with our best fighters on watch." Captain Najat asked. "It's a damn sight shorter than riding the current to Maropret."

There was a murmur of agreement among several of the officers.

Claudio shook his head. "Lurco and Elazaro say the outrigger is not strong enough to attempt. We would snap a spar and set adrift."

"So we scuttle the *Delilah Fritzbink* and use *Pomsta*," I said.

Claudio stared at me with his remaining eye. "That is not an option."

"The cargo, all the farming equipment, is gone," I said. *All the weapons you were smuggling to — where were you smuggling them?*

Claudio snapped his head to Reno who nodded to confirm my assertion.

"Damnation!" Claudio said. With a sigh he asked, "You would sink your grandfather's ship?"

"If it meant we live, yes."

The ship heaved forward, tossed us all against tables and bulkheads. Crew shouted from the deck.

Reno pushed his way through the gathered crowd toward the door to the main deck. "Pirates?"

"How many casters do we have?" Claudio raised his hand.

I raised my hand, as did Najat, Tomas, and the lean Ensign from Laetia.

Reno placed one hand on his sword and the other to the hatch. He pulled open the hatch, and the ship heaved again. One of the three masts of the *Pomsta* slammed into the deck of the *Fritzbink*.

Claudio ran to his quarters and appeared a moment later with an armful of weapons. *Where were those hidden?*

He handed the blades to the officers.

I pushed to the hatch and onto the deck. Sheets and canvas draped over the *Fritzbink*. The crew worked to cut themselves free. From the deck of the *Pomsta* Kane pointed to something aft of the boat.

An enormous black arm reached from the dark water, ten furlongs high. The black tentacle coiled around the *Pomsta's* mizzenmast and snapped it in three places, sent splinters, stays, and canvas raining down on the deck of the sloop.

"Get to the quarterdeck!" Reno shouted, and jumped over the fallen mainmast and climbed on to the broken forecastle. A second black arm reached up over the bow and wrapped around the bowsprit of the *Fritzbink*. A third. A fourth.

"Kraken!" The shout rose from the sloop.

"All crew to arms," I shouted as I climbed the ladder to the quarterdeck. Jabnit held the tiller in one hand and a bright blade he had pilfered from one of the pirates on the beach in the other.

Armed officers poured through the hatch onto the main deck as a black tentacle slammed into the deck, seized the lean Laetian, and lifted him into the air.

A bolt of lightning struck the arm just below the entangled ensign. Reno drew another sigil and a second bolt struck.

I closed my eyes and breathed deep to relax myself and harnessed the *yili* of the sea. The energy welled within me and the threads revealed the massive creature beneath our ships.

A third lightning bolt struck as the arm slammed into the deck once more. It dashed the ensign against the deck, killing him.

I set my *sebi* on the tentacle wrapped around the foremast of the *Pomsta*, our last hope of getting home. With an arcane word, a ball of fire erupted against the arm.

POP.

I rushed the spell. It was inefficient, but the dark finger loosened its grasp on the mast as the canvas burst into flames.

The scorched arm slammed into the deck of the *Pomsta* and raked two sailors off the deck into the dark waters.

"Man overboard!" The shouts rose over the commotion.

I set my *sebi* on the enormous body of the creature, hidden below the ship. I had no idea if it would work, but I had few options remaining.

The battle raging on the deck slowed as I pulled more *yili* into me. Lightning and fire exploded both starboard and larboard as other casters joined the fray.

I spoke the word for lightning and released all the *yili* in my well. A bolt of lightning as wide as the ship split the sky and slammed into the water, setting the sea to a boil. The resulting thunder as the air rushed together knocked everyone off balance. Sailors grabbed their ears as the deafening explosion rocked the ship.

The massive arms tensed. Another loud explosion sounded as the treelike spar of the two outriggers snapped in unison.

Najat leaped from the deck of the *Fritzbink* to her ship as it, now free of the black arms that held it, drifted. She landed hard on the deck of the sloop, rolled, and jumped to her feet.

Two large arms climbed from the water and wrapped around the *Fritzbink* amidship.

The wood of the deck groaned under the intense strain of the Kraken's grip. With three arms forward and three aft, the creature used its ancient strength to pull at the ship.

A frenetic series of lightning bolts struck the creature, but it did not yield. The groan of the timber grew louder as the strain increased. Crew hacked at the tentacles with swords and axes to no avail.

CRACK.

The keel succumbed to the strength of the ancient fiend. Splintered wood exploded from the lower decks as the creature split the *Fritzbink* in two.

There, between the two halves of the ship sailed by three generations of my family, was the legendary horror seen by sailors before their death. The beak-like maw of the Kraken opened as Tomas and Majid tumbled to their demise.

I ducked under a sweeping arm and ran to grab hold of the rail of the doomed ship. Once again, I pulled the *yili* of sea into my being.

A tentacle grabbed hold of Fawz, blade still striking the arm as the beast pulled him to his death.

The Fabric thrummed as I pulled more and more threads. I spoke an arcane word and a bolt of lightning struck the beast in the center of its gaping maw. As the arms seized from the bolt, the final beams of the *Delilah Fritzbink* yielded to the strength of the Kraken and splintered. I fell into the water with the detritus of the ancient ship and prepared myself for my fate.

Silhouetted by the arcane lamps of the ship and the pale moons, just beneath the waves was the grotesque form of the ancient beast. Its massive yellow eyes looked from the side of its head out toward me.

I reached the surface of the waves as the remains of the bow rained down. I clawed my way onto a piece of floating wood and searched for survivors. The light of the *Fritzbink* dimmed beneath the surface. The *Pomsta* was gone, pulled away by the current. The water was dark and cold and silent.

This was my fault.

CHAPTER THIRTY-FIVE

What the hell am I doing here? The greater world is no place for a gnome. This was the life I wanted, wasn't it? The life of adventure.

Waves lapped over the wooden door as I tried to find a safe balance. I couldn't risk falling into the water. *Is that thing still out there? It must be.*

"The world is just too big and too dangerous," Zori would say. "Work on your studies and take over the Empire when you are ready."

I doubt Zori meant the fucking Kraken when she said that. She always had her plan for me.

"Take over the Empire."

"Join the University."

"Help me expand the farm."

Everyone in my family had a plan for me, safe plans that didn't involve dragons hunting me down, that didn't include being accused of a crime I didn't commit.

I killed a man today.

Several. The blade just slid into his body. He was dead, by my hand.

Should I feel remorse for killing him? I don't. It's wrong that I don't feel anything, isn't it? If I hadn't killed him, he would have killed me. It was that simple.

"Gods," the word slipped from my mouth.

The icy wind picked up. It stung against my shivering, wet skin. I balled up in the middle of the splintered door of the *Fritzbink's* head, floating somewhere in the Azurean Sea.

This is how I die. My life of adventure ends on the door to the fucking shitter.

I was supposed to get married next year.

CHAPTER THIRTY-SIX

It was the summer of my thirtieth year, seven since *The Esmerelda* sank, since Dem joined the army. The Commonwealth called upon his unit. Bringing aid to starving farmers in Maropret, he would tell me when he returned the following spring.

Alone in the city for such a milestone, I spent most of the months of Cassia, Cienta, and Resia on a bender so debauched that the poet Primula would write *"O, Where Have Your Daughters All Gone?"* to commemorate the event. I assure you the part about drinking three orcs and a duck under the table was entirely true.

Dukhan collected my pickled remains from Al Tarhib, a luxurious boarding house near the Gilded Hill.

"Father has business in the Stormreach Mountains, and he asked to bring you along," Duk said.

I argued that I was in no condition to travel and still had to see to the welfare of my guests.

"Yersucha cockblock, Duk," I said. "Madam Tuhon wants me to be her gnomedaddy."

"I doubt the proprietor of the Drakkan Trading Company wants you to be," he sighed, "her gnomedaddy."

He motioned to two humans in his entourage who picked me up and carried me toward the door of the boarding house. He motioned to a third, a woman, who approached.

"Find his trousers. We don't need that thing dragging on the ground," the woman nodded and headed toward common room where I had been entertaining.

They carried me, bare-assed, from Al Tarhib and unceremoniously into Duk's waiting carriage. I lay on the floor of the carriage while the two men stood beside the steps. A moment later the woman exited the boarding house and joined me in the carriage. She rejected my slurred solicitation by tossing my trousers at my head.

Duk climbed into the carriage, and the two men took their places on the back. His eyes were wide with horror as he watched me put on my trousers.

"What?" The jostle of the carriage as we rushed through the streets of Drakkas Port toward the Dragon Gate did not sit well with my stomach. "You look worse than I feel, Duk."

"A stark nude Fatin Tuhon just asked if I would be her gnomedaddy since you were leaving." Duk refused to make eye contact, just stared at the empty seat across from him.

Duk's secretary snickered.

"Told you, cockblock."

"How did you run up a seventy-five silver head tab in just three days?"

"I'wassa good party."

"For seventy-five heads the food better have been served by nude elven maidens on golden platters."

I smiled at my brother. Duk was eighty-five when the empire collapsed. At the end of his second century, he had little patience for my antics. His own children were about my age, and he often treated me more as a child than his brother.

"You did not." His voice became shrill when he was stressed.

"That's a great idea," I said. "I'll remember it for next time."

Duk let out a deep sigh. "We need to get you cleaned up. You can't go to the Enclave looking like you have been on a ten-day bender."

"It's been closer to seventy days, so — thank you."

Duk shook his head and sighed.

The secretary leaned her head out of the window of the carriage and shouted, "Merrywood."

"Yip," came from behind me, the driver.

"You will need to look like the youngest son of Ignis and Zori Alsahar when we arrive at the Enclave," Dem said, "not Madam Tuhon's gnomedaddy."

"I thought that was you now."

"I am not," Duk's voice rose an octave in protest.

The carriage passed through the Dragon Gate and was enveloped by a darkness never experienced by the denizens of the city. As the carriage swayed toward Merrywood, and Duk rambled on, I fell into a deep slumber.

* * *

The path to the Dwarven Enclave of Stormreach was a road little bigger than the carriage which ran along a high cliff. I pressed myself into the seat, careful not to look out the window, and took a swig of whiskey. The better part of the last three days of travel was a drunken haze. Ignis met us at Merrywood the morning after Duk and I arrived. They tossed me into a bath, after which I shaved, and dressed in Duk's clothes, constricting and uncomfortable.

By midday we were on our way toward the Stormreach Mountains with a considerable entourage: servants; drivers; guards; Duk's personal secretary, Orlina; and five scholars from the University eager to gain access to the reclusive Enclave for a few days.

As we passed through the massive stone gates of the Enclave's outer walls, we found the ancient

265

mountain city decorated for festivity. Crimson and gold flags of the Commonwealth were a stark contrast to the cloudy gray skies.

I thought the flags, banners, and bunting odd, since everything I had ever read about the dwarves showed they were a fierce warrior culture with little interest in festivities that didn't involve bloodshed.

"They won't make me fight, will they?"

"It's not that kind of event," Duk said.

The carriage pulled through the gates of Pallinar, the palace of the famed King of the Enclave. Just beyond the rising bronze domes of Pallinar, the Great Spire pierced the thick grey clouds.

My father stepped from the carriage, and a burly dwarf with a beard the same color of the clouds embraced the elder gnome. My brother followed, and the dwarf gave him the same reception.

"Here we go." I handed my drink to the Orlina, took a deep breath, and took the two steps of the carriage with grace and poise.

Duk's carriage, however, had three steps. I clipped my heel on the final rung. The cumbersome clothes Duk had dressed me in made any form of maneuvering impossible. I tumbled face first into the stone at the foot of the dwarf who let out a deep laugh before offering a hand.

"Ofta great start, lad. Least Lulu wasn't here to see it. Auch, ye got a bitta red on ye." The dwarf offered me a cloth to wipe the blood away. "Ye wee ones break so easy."

Duk rolled his eyes, then spoke in a near falsetto, "Balfour, we appreciate you inviting us."

I know that name. Why did I know that name?

"Well, s'not mah decision to make," Balfour said. "But it might be a short trip fer ye."

Duk's sharp breath blew two clouds of steam from his nostrils like a dragon. Even in the summer the Enclave was at an elevation that remained cold year round.

"Has Remus made it back?" Duk's voice raised another octave.

"Won't make it, sadly. He's headed to Maropret," Balfour said as he led us into Pallinar. "C'mon, let's get ye some drink and calm ye nerves. Any higher, Duk, and the dogs'll be howling."

Balfour led us through the wide stone hallways of Pallinar to a spacious room decorated with a menagerie of taxidermy creatures, large comfortable chairs, and a massive stone fireplace. With drinks in hand, Duk, Ignis, and Balfour set to discussing Drakkan politics while I perused the library.

A turn after we arrived in the great room, a young dwarven woman entered, flanked by attendants. Perhaps only eighteen years old, she wore a green dress in the traditional dwarven style. She had green eyes that sparkled in the firelight, brilliant red hair, and a short, braided beard.

We all stood as she entered the room.

Balfour walked over the young dwarven woman and kissed her forehead. "Allow me to present my daughter, Lusia Stormjaw, Princess of the Reach. Lulu, this is Professor Ignis Alsahar and his sons Dukhan and Ferrin."

Ignis and Duk gave a nod of respect to the young woman.

I raised my glass in salute, "Princess."

Ignis slumped and rubbed his temples. Balfour's face soured, but regained his composure. "Lulu, would ye like to show Ferrin the gardens?"

* * *

By the time we returned from our walk, four turns had passed. As we entered the great hall, I could hear the talk of politics as though we had just left. *How are they still at it?*

"Well?" Balfour asked with a practiced look of pained understanding already on his face.

Lusia looked to her father with a smile, "I like him. He could be fun to break."

Balfour raised his eyebrows in genuine surprise, "Are ye sure?"

"It is so," she said.

Balfour nodded, "Well then, it is so."

"It is so," I echoed. "Just don't call me gnomedaddy."

Lusia let out a delicate chuckle, "Daen't worry about that."

Duk's voice returned to a falsetto, "And with that, we should retire for the evening."

"Right." Balfour looked at me over once more, then turned to Ignis. "We'll sort out the specifics later."

Ignis nodded and several dwarven attendants led us to a comfortable suite of rooms where we found the rest of our entourage.

The following morning, the reason for Ignis's trip sorted while I was away, we prepared to leave for Drakkas Port. Lusia did not appear to send us off, as I hoped she would, but Balfour was there with a large toothy grin. He embraced us each and waved as our carriage departed.

When we passed through the massive stone gates of the Enclave, Duk turned to address me, "What in ten hells did you say on that walk?"

"We talked about Pallum and the history of the city," I said. "She was impressed by how much of the history I knew. We talked about life at the University. She's attending now. Things like that."

"Well, at any rate, congratulations, Fer," Duk said. He poured a healthy glass of whiskey and placed it in my hands.

"On what? Not making a fool out of you? Did you sort out whatever you came here for? I was expecting to be there for a few days."

"Ten gods among us, Ferrin, did you listen to anything I said on the way here?"

"As little as possible, Duk." I took a swig of the whiskey.

"Congratulations on your engagement to Princess Lusia, son," Ignis said.

I spat my drink out, covering Ignis and Orlina in a fine mist of the eighteen-year-old whiskey. I coughed as the liquor burned my throat. "My what?!"

"King Balfour agreed to let Lusia consider you as a suitor. The wedding won't be until after she completes her studies at the University," Duk said.

"Which will be in three to five years," Ignis added.

"But what of Madam Tuhon?"

"To the hells with Tuhon," Duk shouted, his voice raising in pitch.

"Dwarves are surprisingly comfortable with extramarital relations," Ignis said. "Do whatever you wish to Tuhon, but once your mother finds out, expect to be caught *in flagrante*."

CHAPTER THIRTY-SEVEN

I was adrift, alone on that door for days. I discovered a wooden tankard floating on the waves. It took days of trial and error before I discovered the arcane words to desalinate the seawater.

The nights grew longer. It would soon be Nexis soon, if it wasn't already. This far north the sun might not rise over the horizon for spans.

Each time a piece of wood drifted close enough to reach, I fastened it to the door with a strip of cloth from my shirt.

When night came, I recited the same prayer:

Commander Ferrin Alsahar of Drakkas Port died in service the Southern Empire Trading Company. Though we commit his body to the deep, we ask

Lady Nex to guide his spirit to a peaceful slumber. Blessings upon you, Father, Lord of the Deep. I am but a humble sailor, cast upon your waves. Lord Aequor, god of the seas, I have offered you everything I have but my life. I humbly ask that you watch over me. Protect me, until the day you call me home. Perhaps this is that day.

* * *

Eleven days after the Kraken pulled the *Delilah Fritzbink* beneath the waves a large chunk of mast moved close enough to my raft for me to grab hold of it. Draped over the spar was the body of a man, Claudio. I pulled the mast section to the raft; he groaned as the waves jostled him.

He was alive!

I pulled Claudio onto my raft of debris, closed my eyes and pulled the *yili* of the sea into me and felt stronger, more alive, than I had in days. I set my *sebi* on the captain and spoke the words I learned in Tomas's book. The energy of the sea flooded into the near-dead man. I held him so he wouldn't roll into the water. He inhaled and coughed.

"Where?" it was all he got out.

"No idea, drifting east for the last eleven days," I handed him my tankard of fresh water.

He slurped it down and opened his eyes. "Still you," he said with a sigh.

"Sorry to disappoint."

He laughed. "Could be worse."

"Than floating adrift on the open sea after the Kraken ripped your ship apart and left you for dead?"

"When you put it like that."

I laughed.

"Do you have anything to eat?"

"Occasionally a fish will move close enough to surface to grab."

"Reno, you taught him so much, but nothing useful," Claudio said. He closed his eyes for a moment. At first, I thought he had fallen asleep, then he shouted an arcane phrase in a graveled, broken voice. A large fish materialized in his open hands.

My eyes widened. I had subsisted off bait fish for a span. With a word Claudio had conjured a feast.

✳ ✳ ✳

After fifteen days adrift, sails appeared on the horizon. I used all the energy I had to will the current toward the ship.

As the sails grew larger on the horizon, Claudio conjured a bright, colored flare above us.

The ship, a sloop from Maropret headed toward Whyte Harbor, hoisted its sails and pulled us from the water.

They were certain we were dead. The crew had found several corpses along the voyage, along with the debris of several destroyed ships. They dragged us aboard, and gave us food, water, and dry blankets. I found a comfortable spot on their deck and fell asleep for what seemed like days.

CHAPTER THIRTY-EIGHT

There was a knock at the door of the cabin Claudio and I shared. A young human boy, no older than Cort, opened the door without waiting for a reply.

"Captain Azpa, Sergeant Leon, the captain said to tell you we will arrive in Whyte Harbor in about a turn," the boy said. He withdrew as quick as he entered, off to continue his tasks.

"Of all the names—"

"His was on the manifest."

"There were others."

"No one would believe for a moment you were a deckhand."

I snorted at the accusation.

We had been aboard the *King Ta'Ruh* for twenty-five days. Claudio, ever cautious of my capture, identified me as his first mate, Reno Leon. The crew dismissed my confusion when they called me by the name of my dead shipmate. Two spans on the open ocean without food or water can do that.

Even now, a month under the assumed name, my stomach still knotted to hear it.

We had no personal items to collect, the notification was more a formality in our case. Captain Franciz Isem would report her two castaways to the Harbor Master as the law required her. The Watch would want to interview us, verify we weren't victims of a mutiny.

"As soon as the gangplank is across, we make our way to the Empire," I ran through our plan one last time.

"With any luck, the station manager here will be competent enough to help us evade more prying questions," Claudio said.

"What if the army is still patrolling the harbor?"

"Then we will just have to improvise," he said. "Ready?"

I nodded.

Claudio and I left the cabin and climbed the narrow ladder to the deck of the *Ta'Ruh*. The Whyte Citadel perched like a beacon high atop the island just off our bow.

We joined Captain Isem and navigator Ensign Vela at the tiller. I studied the shape of the Citadel.

No dragons perched atop the battlements, a good sign.
Just below the Citadel was the bulk of the city, a few
temples, the telltale trappings of a marketplace, and
a thick cluster of houses. Along the harbor rose large
trading houses and lines of warehouses along the
waterfront. *No walls.*

The icy water lapped against the hull of the sloop.
Much like the *Pomsta*, the deck of the *Ta'Ruh* was low
to the waterline with three masts along her
centerline. Her sleek profile and light displacement
helped with fast runs between islands—fast being a
relative term. The *Fritzbink*, for example, had a deep
draft and the power of a single sail. She could never
run against the Azurean Current on her own, even
with two casters filling her canvas the entire route.

Our return trip from Whyte Harbor, had things
gone to plan, would have taken us around Whyte
Harbor and down the western side of the
archipelago which dotted the map from Drakkas
Port to Whyte Harbor.

No sooner than when the mooring line met the
iron cleat did we bid farewell to Captain Isem. We
reminded her again she could find us at the Empire.
Returning two Empire crewmen, officers no less, to
port would earn her and her crew a comfortable
payment from Zori.

The harbor was a tangle of people from all ports
moving with the same swiftness of Dockside. I
followed Claudio as he pushed through the crowds

and attempted to stay clear of the Watch and the Harbor Master's tower.

"Have you thought about where you will go next?" Claudio chatted nervously as he maneuvered the throngs of people.

After all of this, I wanted to go home. "Drakkas Port," I said.

"You will face certain imprisonment if you return, no?"

"Whatever I face there, it is far better than what I've experienced," I said, "storms, pirates, the fucking Kraken!"

Claudio just laughed.

I fixated on one ship, near the quay wall: a vessel crafted of dark timbers and an unusual design. The markings on her hull were out of place, neither Imperial nor Drakkan. A sailor came from below decks on the strange ship. He was pale-skinned with golden hair. That's when I realized the markings were in Eisiger. *This was a Nivalean ship.* My heart raced. *Had the pirates come here? No, that was ridiculous. They must be traders from the northern continent.*

Claudio turned at the sea wall and followed a line of warehouses.

"You said you wanted adventure, my friend," Claudio continued his conversation again as we pushed closer together around stevedores with carts of cargo. "What life is waiting for you back home? Even if the Watch does not throw you into prison?

"My life," I said.

"Sharing someone else's tales in a seedy tavern? Bedding barmaids and merchants' daughters?" Claudio laughed. "You could do that in any land, as a free man! And they would be your own stories to tell."

We reached a towering building with a familiar crest above the door, The Southern Empire Trading Company.

"Just something to think about," Claudio said as he pushed open the polished oak door of the trading house.

"Good morning, gentle — ten hells you are dead!" The thin clerk behind the desk leaped to his feet, and rushed toward the both of us.

"We are not dead, Barnaby, just — detained," Claudio said opening his arms to embrace the clerk.

Barnaby ducked under Claudio's arms and ran to the door, hefted a large oak plank and slid it into iron brackets on either side of the frame, barricading the door. He turned back to us.

"You don't understand. You are dead," he panted as he ducked under Claudio's still outstretched arms and back to his desk. "I filed the paperwork a month ago. The Harbor Master declared the *Delilah Fritzbink* lost in that massive storm back in Panis."

The clerk shuffled documents on his desk, searching for something, perhaps proof we were not permitted to still be alive. He paused and looked at the two of us. Claudio put his arms down, resigned to the fact his clerk had declared him dead and was not happy to see us debating the fact.

"Did you know the army came here?" He looked up from his paperwork with wide eyes. "They said they had warrants for the arrest of Gustavo Blanco, an alias for Ferrin Alsa — oh shit. No. No, no, no." The clerk had connected the dots, identifying the strange gnome standing next to one of his captains.

"It's pronounced Alsahar," I said.

"They brought a dragon! And a column of soldiers from the Citadel. I don't know what you did, but they sat in this room for two spans until the Harbor Master declared all hands on the *Fritzbink* lost."

Claudio took a deep breath. "The Harbor Master may have been premature in that declaration," Claudio said. The clerk opened his mouth, but the captain raised a finger. "But all souls aboard the *Delilah Fritzbink* perished, save myself and Reno Leon." Claudio emphasized the name as he pointed in my direction. "The same for the crews of the *Kestrel's Wing,* the *Azurean Strela,* and the *Pomsta.*"

The clerk furrowed his brow for a moment, then nodded a slow understanding.

"I suspect you received a letter from Zori some time after the army arrived, yes?" It was the question that wasn't a question Claudio was so skilled in delivering.

Another furrowed brow, followed by a look of recognition — the clerk ran through the door behind his desk into the warehouse area. A moment later he rolled a wooden chest reinforced with iron bands into the room.

Barnaby stopped the chest in front of Claudio and I, then produced a brass key on a chain from around his neck. He handed me the key and hurried back to the desk.

"Go ahead," Claudio urged. "Open it. It is for you."

I slid the key into the lock and pushed the lid of the chest open. Inside was a set of exquisitely crafted leather armor with a dragon carved into the cuirass. The armor was smaller than any I had ever seen before, almost like someone designed it for a child.

Or a gnome.

I lifted the cuirass out of the chest. Beneath the armor was a pair of steel daggers wrapped in linen, a rucksack with two sets of well-made traveling clothes, a gray wool cloak with pockets hidden inside the lining, and a pair of sturdy leather boots.

At the bottom of the chest was a leather satchel with my family name embroidered in gnomish. Inside the pouch was a letter and scroll with the seal of the Drakkan Commonwealth. My hands shook.

I sat on the floor of the trading house and read the letter scrawled in neat gnomish characters:

> *My Dearest Ferrin,*
>
> *If you are reading this, my worst fears have come to pass. A group of unknown people have attempted to unseat me from the Council of Lords*

*and have attacked you to achieve their goals. But
you have escaped to safety.*

*Drakkas Port is no longer safe for you. The
Commonwealth is no longer safe for you. You
must flee. I can not bear the thought of harm
coming to you, my son. The station manager has
provided you with everything you need to start a
new life beyond the Commonwealth and will
guarantee you passage to anywhere in the world.*

*You are so charming, and I know you will thrive
wherever you go. I will come find you when this
threat is behind us.*

Stay safe my love,

Zori

I looked up from the letter. Tears filled my eyes.
Claudio had pulled on a fresh tunic and a pair of
sabers from somewhere in the office and searched
through a ledger as Barnaby reappeared holding a
small chest, about the size of a large tome.

"You are in luck. I was about to send this back to
the home office in the morning." The clerk placed the
chest on the floor next to me, "as instructed."

My hands shook as I fumbled for the latch. This
was all too much to process. Inside the chest was
row upon row of golden coins placed on a red velvet
tray. Next to the stacks of coins was a small pouch
filled with gemstones.

"Five hundred gold anchors and assorted stones
that can be converted into any currency," he said in a
tone far too comfortable for what he has just handed
me, "roughly one hundred ships total."

Claudio gave a low, breathy whistle. "You could buy your own fleet with that."

"It's our earnings from last month," Barnaby said. "By sending it with you and a report of nothing earned, the home office would send someone to investigate. They could pass a message without the chance of it being intercepted. At least, that's the only reason I could think to give you everything. What did the letter say?"

"I have to get back to Drakkas Port," I said. "When does the next ship leave?"

I put the small chest in the bottom of the rucksack and put on the new clothes and boots. I thought for a moment, then donned the armor. It was a comfortable fit.

"Our next ship to Drakkas Port leaves with the tide tomorrow morning," Barnaby said.

"And you can make sure I, Reno, whoever, is scheduled to be aboard?"

"Of course."

"Good," Claudio said with a smile. "Then we should get food. I am famished."

At the thought of food my stomach roared to life. The food had been dry rations aboard the *Ta'Ruh*. My mouth watered at the prospect of an actual meal. I draped the cloak over the armor, placed the daggers into the rucksack and slung it over my shoulder.

"If the Watch comes looking for us, we will be at the Dragon and Eagle down the street," Claudio said as he lifted the oak plank from the door.

"The Watch?" Barnaby asked with renewed panic. It seemed to be his natural state.

"We were castaways," Claudio said. "Which reminds me, you owe Captain Isem of the *King Ta'Ruh* for our rescue and passage."

"Oh good," Barnaby said.

Claudio pushed me through the door and out into the street. "There is something I need you to see."

✳ ✳ ✳

The Dragon and Eagle looked no different from any of the other establishments we passed on our way. Claudio opened the door and motioned for me to enter.

The Dragon and Eagle prided themselves on being a tavern for officers, not a just another seedy dockside pub. There was a dress code Rosalyn, the owner and bartender, enforced. As such, patrons were met by a floor-to-ceiling mirror to ensure their appearance would meet Rosalyn's exacting standards.

"What do you see?" Claudio leaned close so only I could hear him.

Before me stood a gnome with skin darkened and creased from endless days in the unforgiving Azurean sun. A scar ran from his disheveled black hair, down his right cheek, to his thick, dark beard.

He wore matching leather armor that peeked from under his gray cloak. His eyes were dark, sunken, with a stare that had seen more than any man should.

"I see," I said just above a whisper, "an adventurer."

CHAPTER THIRTY-NINE

"Captain Azpa," Rosalyn greeted Claudio with the warmth of an old friend. "You look like you fell through all ten hells. Who is your friend?"

"Turns out, there is an eleventh, Ros. Oh, and I am, in fact, dead."

"You look it," Ros said with a snort. "So your spirit is here to settle your tab?"

"We are here to celebrate the lieutenant's promotion."

"Ah! Congratulations, Lieutenant," Ros said. "You want your usual table, Captain?"

Ros didn't bother to wait for a response. Instead she walked toward a curtained off area near the back of the common room.

"Come here often?" I looked up to the disheveled seaman.

"In a city full of merchant and sailors, you have to do something special to attract the best clientele. In Whyte Harbor that would be ships' officers." Claudio slid into a polished wooden booth. "Ros, here, specializes in meals from home."

Whose home?

"Beef Callumine, as usual?" Ros asked. The captain nodded his approval.

"How about a nice spiced lamb roast for you, Lieutenant?" Ros slid into Drakkan with such a command of the language it took me a moment to realize she had changed tongues.

I nodded. Ros turned from the booth and released the curtain to conceal the table from the rest of the room.

"Did she?" I fumbled for words. Claudio laughed at my response.

"As best as I counted, she can speak over a dozen languages," Claudio said. "It pains her to not greet you in Gnomish. She will at least have the basics the next time you …"

Claudio paused, then looked down at the table. His warm smile fled.

"Have you decided where you will go?" He changed the subject.

"I have to get back home," I said. "Zori said someone was trying to unseat her from the Council of Lords."

I paused. *Zori was one of the Lords of Drakkas Port?*

It was obvious Claudio had the same thought. His eyebrows shot up at the mention of the Council. "I — I suppose that would make sense in a way," he said. "She is the most powerful merchant in the Commonwealth. If that is true, then you are in more danger than I could imagine. It would also explain why the accusations against you were so significant."

"How much more danger?"

"Do you recall reading about the collapse of the empire a century ago in your studies?"

"Sure, Zori and Ignis were there," I said, "my brother as well."

"If someone is trying to overthrow a Commonwealth Lord — a hidden lord at that — this is not revenge. It is a coup."

I ran my fingers through my hair. "What would you do?"

"An unknown enemy with powerful connections," he said, "powerful enough to take on Zori Alsahar — I would run."

We sat in silence for a time as I considered what he said.

Eventually he spoke again. "What am I doing? This is supposed to be a celebration."

He reached under the table and came back up holding one of the two sabers he had pilfered from the Company office.

"What's this? It's as large as I am," I said with a chuckle. "How were you even sitting here with that on?"

"When a captain decides a midshipman has completed his training and is ready to serve on his own, he presents the midshipman with a saber, a symbol of authority and rank as an officer," he said. "You have done more in two months than some midshipmen will do in years of training. So I am presenting you with your saber."

"Claudio, I—" tears welled up in my eyes.

The curtain shifted, and we silenced our conversation. I slung the saber belt over my torso and across my chest. Ros moved the curtain with her elbow and placed a platter of still sizzling meat in front of each of us.

She ducked out of the curtain and returned a moment later with a full bottle of Stormreach Whiskey and two glasses. "You said you were celebrating, right?"

Her Drakkan was perfect.

My damp eyes widened to the size of my platter at the sight of the bottle. *Had it been two months? It felt as though years had passed.*

"It is a celebration!"

She dropped the bottle and glasses on the table. "Well then, enjoy!" she said. "To the Empire!"

I reached up and poured myself three fingers of the amber elixir into a glass. The aroma of the liquor and the spiced roast wrapped me in the memories of home.

We did not say another word until both our platters were clear and two thirds of the bottle was empty.

"I have a friend," Claudio broke the silence first. "She is a former captain with the Company and takes on contract work from time to time. Her ship, the *Harpy's Remorse,* had a manifest in the Empire office when we arrived."

I furrowed my brow. Now well intoxicated, I couldn't decide the captain's intention with the remark.

"I added our names." He cleared his throat, "the names of Claudio Azpa and Reno Leon, to the manifest. She sails tonight for the west coast of Nivalis."

"Claudio, we were in a shipwreck—two shipwrecks. I have no interest in Nivalis," I said with all the sternness I could muster. "I want to go back to Drakkas Port. Whatever is waiting for me there, it can't be any worse than what we've experienced so far."

Claudio huffed then nodded. "This whiskey is stronger than I remember. I need to hit the head. Think about it."

He pulled the curtain aside to reveal a now bustling common room and marched toward the back of the tavern.

Two large humans seated at a table close to our shrouded booth huddled close together and looked in my direction more than once.

"And what do you two want?" It was a drunken shout that drew the attention of a few patrons.

"My mate here," said the bearded of the two men. "Said he heard you mention a shipwreck, said he was looking for a bloke on a ship that was lost, the *Delilah Fritzbink*. Was that your ship?"

I sobered as he spoke my grandmother's name. "Sorry, mate, I was on the *Pomsta*."

Not a complete lie.

The two stood and moved closer to the curtained table. "You see, the thing is, we have been looking for a gnome," said the clean-cut man.

"Just like you," his bearded partner said.

"Who was lost at sea in a shipwreck," Cleancut said.

"Just like you," Beard added.

"And may be on his way back to Whyte Harbor," Cleancut said.

"So here we are," Beard said.

With a third of a bottle of the strongest whiskey on any shore coursing through my veins, my reaction time was slower than it should have been. In all honesty, I let my guard down and it bit me in the ankle.

The two mercenaries (and by their odor they were mercenaries) grabbed me, threw me over Beard's shoulder, grabbed my rucksack, and were out the door before I had time to realize what happened. The sun was already dipping below the horizon. In a mark the narrow streets would be dark. I shouted as the two escaped into an alley beside the Dragon and Eagle.

Claudio was still relieving himself in the alley behind the tavern. He heard the commotion and ran toward me and my latest captors.

"Unhand that officer of the Southern Empire," he said.

Cleancut laughed, tossed my rucksack against the urine-soaked wall, and drew a sword, "What are you going to do about it, Eyepatch?"

Beard threw me to the ground with a swift kick to the stomach, "Stay put if you know what's good for you."

Claudio reached for his sabers. He patted the spot where the blade he had given me had been. With a flourish, he pulled his lone saber and blocked a chopping strike from Cleancut and pushed him into Beard.

Claudio turned and put himself between me and my would-be captors. Cleancut untangled himself from Beard and rushed in for another attack. Claudio parried the strike, but Beard used the distraction to drive a dagger into Claudio's side.

The three men slowed as I pulled *yili* from their motion.

"No," Claudio shouted. "The Watch will find you."

POP.

The Fabric thrummed as I released the energy I built within myself.

Claudio grabbed Beard's wrist and kicked him toward me, sending both the captain and the mercenary off balance. Claudio fell to one knee. Blood seeped from between his fingers against his chest.

No.

The mercenary stumbled my direction. I pulled my saber, planted my feet, and plunged the weapon between the mercenary's shoulder blades. Torchbearer stance. The saber reappeared through the front of Beard's chest as he let out gurgled scream before he collapsed to the ground.

I looked to Claudio who was now on the ground. Cleancut saw his companion bleeding out on the cobbles of the alley. He shouted something in a language I didn't recognize.

"That's no way to talk about anyone's mother," a voice behind the mercenary said.

"Ten hells, what's going on back here?" another voice asked. This one more feminine.

I tightened my grip on the now crimson blade and changed my stance to Greedy Goblin. *Great, more mercenaries.*

As I shifted positions, I could see an elf and an orc behind Cleancut. The large mercenary charged toward me. For a brief second, I heard an arcane word, then nothing.

A massive blade exploded through Cleancut's mouth as the orc pantomimed a ferocious roar. The body of the mercenary slumped on the end of the blade. The orc lowered blade, and the body slid to the ground next to his companion. With gesture from the orc, the elf waved his hand and released the enchantment.

"What did you do to get the Red Hand after you, little one?" the orc asked as she shook the blood from the enormous blade and slid it into the sheath on her back.

I rushed to Claudio's side. His breath was shallow as blood pooled near his body. I closed my eyes and sought the *yili* within him. There was only a faint flicker of light, a dim yellow that sputtered to remain alight.

"I need to help him," I said.

I focused and bound his wounds.

Claudio grabbed my wrist. "This is not the life you want, my friend," his voice was coarse as he strained to speak. "Go now. Captain Keets waits for you."

"Of all the boats in the ocean, we are on our way to Keets," the elf said.

"And we're late," the orc added.

"Well I don't think he minds that we stopped," the elf nodded toward me.

I tried again to find Claudio's *yili*, but his face was stern. I stepped back from Claudio and grabbed my rucksack from against the alley wall. I pulled two daggers from the belt of the dead merc and slid them into my own.

It was then I noticed a rolled-up piece of parchment in Beard's pocket. Something compelled me. I needed to read it. I reached down, pulled the roll, and read what the mercenaries died to claim.

Wanted for Murder and Treason

FERRIN ALSAHAR

Drakkan Gnome, Last seen aboard the Trading Ship Delilah Fritzbink.

One Hundred Silver Heads for his live capture and return to Drakkas Port.

Fifty Silver Heads for proof of his death.

By order of the Lord Protector of the Commonwealth.

My blood ran cold.

"I will not tell you again," Claudio said. He braced himself against the urine-soaked wall as he tried to stand. "I will live, thanks to you. Now you must do the same."

"We should get going," the orc said. "This is the last ship north before the ice."

With the bloody warrant still in my hands, I followed the two travelers from the dark alley.

CHAPTER FORTY

E very summer since I had first picked up an instrument, I had spent in the streets of Drakkas Port performing for crowds and travelers as they passed by, with hopes I could gather enough money to buy beers for the Dem and I that evening.

Dem set up his easel in the Market District and often spent his days trying to convince pretty girls to sit with him while he drew their likeness in charcoal.

The summer past my twenty-third year was hot, and the first day with clouds in the sky coincided with the start of Cassis's feast days. Most of the city had gone to Fort Hydrus to see exhibitions of fighting and watch gladiators and soldiers battle in the war god's temple.

The serpentine paths through the merchant stalls in the Grand Arcade fell silent as worshipers and revelers settled in for five days of drinking, fighting, and drinking.

Lacking of an audience, I went in search of Dem in hopes we could find something better to do with our time. My hopes were high that would include women and alcohol.

I sat next to Dem while he worked on a sketch of an empty stall in the Grand Arcade. Drawn by Dem's creative endeavors, Erista's muses struck as I stared out toward the harbor.

"What if we took a ship and headed off on an adventure?"

Dem looked up from his charcoal drawing with a face of abject horror and true disgust.

"What?"

"What do you mean, 'what?'" he said. "Do you have any idea how stupid that sounds?"

"Very? Judging by your response."

"Do you have any idea how many laws we would break just by stepping foot on a ship that does not belong to us?"

"Technically, most of the ships in the harbor belong to my family," I said. "So we wouldn't be stealing, just borrowing a ship that my family owns. Without asking. Or telling them we took it."

"Well then let's just go ahead and steal a ship!" Dem said as he rolled up his papers and placed them into his satchel.

"Are you sure?"

"No!" Dem said. He slapped his hand down on his easel. "This is the dumbest idea you have come up with! Worse than the time you decided we should sneak into the Temple District to watch the Eristal Virgins bathe."

"That would have worked."

"Not for a single moment would anyone believe we were there to repair the bathing pool, especially while they were using it!" Dem stood up and folded his easel and stool, nestling them underneath his arm.

Dem neared a fathom tall at this point. I had stopped growing a year after we met, and now I couldn't look him in the eye even if I stood on top of a table.

"Do you have enough money for drinks tonight?" Dem asked.

I reached into my tunic and pulled out my coin purse. It was light, as usual. Three pins and a half knot. "I could swing it, but it would have to be Dockside."

"Dockside works for me. But let's stay away from the Fortress. All the taverns around there raise their prices during feast days."

"The heathens!" I shouted. "A plague upon them. Divine Justice, guide my wrath!"

Dem rolled his eyes, picked up his satchel, and walk down the main thoroughfare toward the docks. "Come along, Divine Justice. We will be late."

"Can you be late to an event you only now decided on?"

"Fine, I want to get there before the crowds let out from the games."

"I have just the place, somewhere the crowds will never go, and the ale is plentiful."

"Sounds like our kind of place. Where are we headed?"

"It's called The Rusted Sextant. It's a sailor's tavern on the west side of the harbor."

Dem stopped mid-stride. "It's not that one that looks like it's about to fall down is it?"

"That's the place!"

"Weren't a few people stabbed in that place just last month?"

"We were contemplating stealing a ship a few moments ago, and now you're worried about a bar fight and a few deaths?"

"WE were not discussing stealing a ship," Dem shouted. "YOU were discussing stealing a ship. I am not stealing a ship. You don't even know how to steer a ship. How are you planning to get it away from the dock?"

* * *

"In the matter of the theft and subsequent sinking of the ship known as *The Esmerelda*, I find you guilty," Justiciar Alfons Silverford said.

"Before you sentence my son, your honor, would you allow a mother to speak in her child's defense?" Zori asked.

"Of course, I would consider any mitigating circumstances you wish to provide," the red-clad justiciar said.

"Is it considered theft to take something that belongs to you?" Zori began.

"Of course not," the justiciar said.

"Is it unlawful to be ignorant in your job?"

"Unwise, but not unlawful."

"Then consider that my son is, in fact, the rightful master of the sloop *Esmerelda*. He could not be guilty of stealing a ship that belongs to him," Zori continued.

I tried my best to conceal the surprise on my face at my mother's words.

"And I trust you have the supporting documents to prove that Ferrin Alsahar was the rightful owner of *The Esmerelda* before its departure from the dock?"

"Of course, your honor. I have those documents with me," Zori handed a scroll of parchment to the justiciar.

The middle-aged human read through the documents provided to him by the gnomish merchant. His lips moved as he read, causing his beard to waggle.

"Well," the justiciar said. "It seems Master Alsahar was the rightful owner of *The Esmerelda* at the time of its sinking, and I cannot convict him of stealing his own property."

A large toothy grin crossed my face as I looked to Dem.

"However," the justiciar continued. "Demetric Pictus was not the lawful captain of *The Esmerelda*. As such he is guilty of commanding a ship without authorization from the Harbor Master, unlawful departure without paying harbor fees, and abandoning a derelict ship in the harbor."

"I would have stayed with the ship had the Watch not fished us from the water," Dem said.

"Master Alsahar, I would strongly recommend that you return to the Imperial University and continue your studies," the justiciar said. "Master Pictus, I am sentencing you to conscription in the Drakkan Army. You are to report to Fort Hydrus in no more than two spans. You are to serve the Commonwealth for a term of five years."

My head spun around to look to my mother. I pleaded with her to help Dem as she helped me. Zori nodded to the justiciar, thanked him, and departed toward the Southern Empire trading house. I stood stunned as my mother walked away from the person I considered my brother.

Dem sat in the dirt where he had stood. Tears rolled across his cheek and down his chin.

"Just think about all the adventures you will get to have." I sat next to him.

"I don't want adventures, Fer," he said. "I just want a comfortable bed and a warm meal now and then without having to beg for it."

The following day I walked with Dem down the harbor wall to Fort Hydrus. I stood beside him as he took the Oath of Enlistment. I embraced him, wished him well, and told him the drinks would always be on me.

Dem wiped the tears from his eyes. He nodded to me, turned, and walked into the fortress with his head held high, as a soldier.

The night Dem enlisted I went to The Rusted Sextant by myself to have a drink or four in honor of my friend.

Still hung-over, I awoke after midday in a room inside The Rusted Sextant. On the table next to the bed was a contract for music and entertainment at the tavern five nights per span, signed by me — beside that, a lease for the room and my coin purse filled with coppers and silver.

CHAPTER FORTY-ONE

The streets of Whyte Harbor were just as crowded as Drakkas Port and twice as cold as I ever experienced. I pulled the cloak around me, in part to fend off the bitter winds, and in part to hide the mercenaries' blood on my hands and chest.

The three of us pushed our way through the crowds to the harbor, careful to avoid patrols of the Watch.

"Do we even know where we are going?" the orc asked.

Claudio had given no description of his friend's ship. All I knew was the name.

"The *Harpy's Remorse*," I said. "By the way, I'm Ferrin. Thanks for helping back there."

A mule-drawn wagon pushed between us.

"I'm Ari Shi, and this the demure Rook Ferox," the elf shouted over the mule.

"Ari?" I asked.

He nodded.

"Fuck," Rook said. "By the time we find the ship's berth she'll have been underway for two turns."

"Are you a criminal, Ferrin?" Ari asked as he pushed aside a longshoreman with a barrel and moved closer.

"No," I said. "Not really. Someone accused me of murder, but I didn't do it."

"You killed that guy back there," Ari said.

"Claudio killed him, and she killed the other one. Someone is trying to make my family look bad. They put a bounty on me."

"That explains why the Red Hand were after you," Rook said.

"Who?"

"Mercenaries, elite soldiers for hire," she said. "If you have the gold, they'll get you the glory. I'm guessing they saw an opportunity and took it."

"I can't see a damn thing with all these people," I said. "What makes you say that?"

"They underestimated you and your friend," Rook said.

"I'll say," Ari added.

The Company contracted the Harpy's Remorse to sail to western Nivalis, so it's likely we should find the ship with the other company vessels.

"I think I know where we can find the ship," I said. I wiped the tears from my cheeks and made for the Empire docks.

I walked with determination and was met with the odd stares and a wide berth from stevedores moving cargo to the ships.

The sun had set by the time I reached the Empire docks; the wharf was lit by massive mage lamps, larger versions of the flameless arcane lights we used on the *Fritzbink*. Ten ships lined the Empire's docks.

I stopped crewmen and asked for ship names and destinations. I got three 'fuck offs', six 'your mothers' houses', and a 'you're a little small for a sailor.'

Reading the names on the ships, none were the *Remorse*.

"We're running out of time," Rook said. "We have to find the ship now if we have any hope of getting aboard."

I grabbed the first Company stevedore that passed close enough. "I'm looking for the *Harpy's Remorse*. Where is it?"

His lower lip moved toward his front teeth, prepared for the same greeting I had received from the sailors on my family's ships.

I grabbed him by the pant leg and pulled him toward me.

"If you tell me to fuck off, I will cut your balls off and feed them to you right here in the street," I growled. "I have had a terrible day and just need to find my ship."

I opened the front of my cloak with my free hand to show the bloody cuirass and the belt of daggers. The stevedore's eyes widened, and he pointed the pier next to the one I had searched. "They shove off in two marks," he said.

I released the longshoreman and thanked him. We turned and ran down the seawall to the dock he indicated.

There was only a single ship on the dock, a three-mast caravel. The crew was making final preparations. We walked up to the gangplank, and I announced myself.

"Sergeant Reno Leon, I would like to speak to the captain." The tears formed once more at the mention of the name.

"You're late," a steward hauling crates toward a hatch said.

"We got tangled up with the locals," I said. "May I speak to the captain?"

The steward nodded, set the crates on the deck, and ran to the aft of the ship. He approached a woman in a dark frock coat and pointed in my direction.

"My tits he is!" the woman yelled as she marched toward the gang plank. "Who the fuck are you?"

"Sergeant Leon," I said. "I booked passage on your ship."

"If you're Reno Leon, then I'm the lost Empress of Fortis!" she said. "You're not even half the size of Reno. And who are these two? Where's Captain Azpa. Wasn't he supposed to be with you, Sergeant?"

I looked to my bloody hands, "Claudio — Claudio didn't make it."

Her demeanor changed, "I never mentioned his first name, so I'll give you that. Did you kill him?"

"What? No!" I said. "We got jumped outside a tavern. These two helped me."

I looked down the dock to see if anyone had followed us.

"Who are you, really?" she said. "I want to know everyone on my ship."

I motioned for her to move closer. She raised her eyebrow at me. I took a step toward the captain and whispered, "I'm Ferrin Alsahar, Claudio was helping. Reno died helping me. Ten hells, the entire crew of the *Fritzbink* died helping me."

She nodded. "If Claudio helped you, so will I," she said, "welcome aboard the *Harpy's Remorse*, sir, Captain Helma Keets at your service. Jarret, help this man to his quarters. I expect the full story from you later. And who are you?"

"Ari Shi and Rook Ferox."

"And you're tied up in this too?"

"It seems so," the elf said.

I nodded to the captain as the steward motioned toward the hatch and the ladder below deck.

"All right, let's go. Raise the gangplank and prepare to make sail," Captain Keets shouted.

"Aye, Captain!" The crew responded in unison.

* * *

The *Remorse* was twice the size of the *Fritzbink*. Where most of the lower deck of the *Fritzbink* was a cargo hold, someone converted the *Remorse's* hold into individual cabins for passengers.

As Jarret led the three of us down a narrow corridor to our quarters, I noted the other passengers: a group of five men and three women, each with a shaved scalp and dressed raiments that marked them as members of the Larian Order. A full suit of plate armor on a wooden stand stood in silent vigil in each of their respective cabins while the clerics gathered together, laughed, and played cards in one room.

Jarret motioned to a starboard cabin, "Madam."

Rook took her rucksack off and threw it into the bunk, then took her two-handed sword, wrapped in cloth, and placed it under her rack with ceremonial reverence.

"And you, sir," Jarret nodded to Ari. The elven man stepped into the cabin, placed his pack down, and pulled books out and set them in a pile of books on the table.

Three doors stood at the end of the corridor. One was my cabin, across from it the one for Claudio. Against the aft bulkhead was a hatch and ladder down to the crew quarters and a galley the passengers and officers shared.

"And here you are," the steward said. He pointed to the pitcher of water and basin in the corner. "You should clean up, sir."

I looked in the mirror above the basin. I was a horror to behold. Blood matted my hair and beard. Crimson smears marked my face from where I wiped away tears with my bloody hands. I placed my rucksack at the foot of the bunk and unclasped the cloak. The mercenaries' blood covered my clothes and armor.

The steward raised his eyebrow at my state. "I'll get you another pitcher of water and more rags."

Alone in my room, I pulled off my armor and washed my hands, hair and face. The water basin turned crimson. I pulled off the bloodstained shirt and held it at arm's length. With an arcane word the blood lifted from the cloth and fell to the wooden deck. This was nothing as gruesome as what I had done on the shores of Ledeni. It was a simple incantation, one I learned from the *Medela*. The same used by Biomancers to clean up after bloody patients.

I fell into my bunk, clean and only half dressed, and drifted into a deep sleep as the ship rolled in familiar time with the sea.

* * *

The *Harpy's Remorse* took a circuitous route to Nivalis, as we hopped from island to island collecting packages and letters, delivering parcels, and trading with small communities.

I learned our destination was the port city of Vyspan on the western coast of Nivalis, beyond the Narrows, and one of the few ports still open on the continent.

War was a topic of frequent conversation, both on the ship and in the island villages where we stopped. A massive civil war had erupted on the northern continent and had displaced many Nivaleans. Ari, Rook, even the Larians had personal stories of battles they shared at night as we sailed between the islands.

When it was my turn, I regaled my fellow travelers with tales of surviving the Great Storm, facing down pirates, and my narrow escape from the Kraken.

For once, all the stories I told were my own and did not need a word of embellishment.

* * *

Thirty-five days passed since we left Whyte Harbor when we entered the Narrows. It was the final night of Arkanus, the ten-day celebration to the god of magic. The sun did not bother to rise above the horizon, leaving the world in constant twilight.

I stood on the deck of the *Remorse,* bundled in the furs I purchased off a trapper on one of our island stops.

"Some sort of bear," he told me.

Even with the bearskin cape my hands shook, and each breath I exhaled hung in the air.

Off the starboard side was Nivalis, and many passengers were on deck to get their first look at the continent. I stood abeam, staring off the larboard side as the steep cliffs and tall tower of Callum Heights came into view through the haze.

I pulled my furs close to my chest as I waited to see the thriving encampments of refugees Dem had described.

As the ship moved closer to the fortress on the Laetian side, I could see the Laetian and Drakkan flags flying from the battlements of the tower. The tall cliffs glowed a deep golden color as the pyres worked. The sand glittered in the firelight like glass. Not like glass. As glass.

Bile rose in my throat as I remembered what Reno told me. *We tell our loved ones what they need to hear sometimes because we could never bear what they would think of us if they knew the truth.*

The horrible truth was a punch to the gut.

Lines of scorched structures stood as a testament to where the dragons had attacked the encampments. The dragon fire burned so hot it turned the sand along the shore into glass.

Large fortifications sat higher on the shore, filled with thousands of the pale-skinned Nivaleans. Laetian soldiers carted the dead from the cages to the funeral pyres. Others tossed the bodies like cord wood onto the fires which flared with each corpse added.

Brother Oswald, the leader of the Larians, stood next to me on the larboard rail. He gripped the railing so hard the skin on his knuckles split in the frigid air. Blood ran down his fist and into the dark waters.

"I—I didn't think it was true," he said.

"Hey kid," Rook said behind me. She adjusted the straps on her breastplate as she approached. "Captain Keets says we should put on armor if we want to stay top—what in the ten hells is that?"

Hot tears rolled down my cheeks.

"The pride of Drakkan ingenuity and the brainchild of my dearest friend, Dem," I said with disgust. "This is Camp Carnum, one of the three extermination camps the Drakkans set up for the Laetians to use on the Nivalean."

Rook stood aghast, the light from the pyres flickered in her eyes. "My gods."

CHAPTER FORTY-TWO

"You expect an answer to everything here, I know," Ferrin said to the panel of justiciars.

"Ye did say we'd have one," Lusia said.

"And you will," the gnome said. He looked around the chamber and noticed the crowd had grown since he started. Soldiers, scribes, and scholars packed into the hall and sat in rapt silence. "It's just that—it's complicated. More complicated than what happened at Callum Heights. We allowed that to happen, and so much worse."

The sky had grown dark. Flames and cinders, the remains of the Grand Arcade, licked up into the night air and illuminated the city. Ferrin turned from the stone arched window toward the panel of red-clad judges. Tears welled in his eyes.

"This might be a good place to stop for the night," he said.

"There's just one thing I 'ave to know before we adjourn for the evening," Lusia said. "If ye loved Dem as much as ye claim, why did ye kill him, Fer?"

The gnome looked down at his hands, at the dried blood that caked them.

"It's what I found next," Ferrin said. "I learned the truth about Dem, the Commonwealth, and who the real traitors are."

There was a murmur from the gallery of those gathered to listen. Several of the justiciars gathered on the dais leaned together and made furious gestures to each other.

Lusia leaned back and stroked her beard with thoughtful consideration of the gnome's admission. She raised an eyebrow and stared at the gore-covered soldier standing in the center of the chaos, both here in the Imperial Hall and in the city beyond the walls of the Black Keep.

After a moment, she gave a knowing nod. "It's late. We'll pick up there in the morning."

The crimson-clad dwarf rose from the chair at the center of the dais. As she stood, the other justiciars took their place by her side.

"If there's nothing else, I'll 'ave two of my men escort ye to yer chambers," Lusia nodded to the guards at either side of Rook and Ari. "Goodnight, my husband."

"Wait. What?" Ferrin said.

"I knew it!" Ari shouted.

"What?"

ACKNOWLEDGMENTS

First, thank you to my wonderful partner, Kristi. Your patience and support helped me beyond measure. Your massive library, suggestions, and insight helped me to fully realize the many cultures and inhabitants surrounding the Azurean Sea.

Thank you to Jeremy, Kathryn, Joss, and Rick for your insights on the many incarnations of the story. I owe you so many beers. To Derek, Jeff, Meagan, and Kristi for sharing a wild idea to play *Dungeons & Dragons* in our 30s. The backstory of my character laid the foundation for Ferrin, Drakkas Port, and this series of books. Thanks as well to the folks at Wizards of the Coast and Critical Role for the inspiration and reminding us all it's okay to dream of dragons.

I would like to thank Chris Fox, Joanna Penn, Derek Murphy, Michael Anderle, Craig Martelle, Mark Dawson, Jenna Moreci, Vivien Reis, the wonderful, supportive Facebook group 20Booksto50k, SPF Podcast, and SFFM Podcast for sharing your insight and expertise with the world and helping independent authors succeed.

Finally, I would like to thank you, the reader, for taking a chance on an unknown author and a story about a gnome on the run. If you are reading this, it hopefully means you enjoyed the novel. You are the reason I wrote this story and I hope you will enjoy the next part of the adventure.

Onward to Nivalis!

A HUMBLE REQUEST

Once again, thank you for reading this book. I truly hope you enjoyed the time spent in this world and look forward to many more adventures. I'm already working on the next one.

I have a humble request. If you have a moment, please leave a rating and review on Amazon about this book. Share the book on the social media. Recommend it to a friend who you think would enjoy it.

Reviews help other readers sort through the millions of books to find the few they might enjoy. For independent authors, such as myself, feedback from readers means everything. We write for the love of the stories and share that passion with you.

Thank you,

Rye

ABOUT THE AUTHOR

Rye has been a fan of the fantasy genre for pretty much his entire life. Books, films, and video games with new and exciting worlds always captured Rye's attention. While other children listened to nursery rhymes, Rye's mother used to read Tolkien. (seriously!)

Rye was multi-award-winning broadcast and online journalist covering everything from high profile crimes to local politics. (Occasionally, in the same story.) After a decade in news, Rye went back to school and earned an MBA. Rye now lives in Mississippi, the land of storytellers, with his partner and their dog.

The *Drakkan Chronicles* is his first foray into fiction.

www.ryesobo.com
www.facebook.com/ryesobo
@ryesobo on Instagram and Twitter

RYE SOBO

Manufactured by Amazon.ca
Bolton, ON